Smiley

and the

Acorn

A Story From Cornwall

ROGER UNDERWOOD

26/8/2021

The right of Roger Underwood to be identified as the author of this work has been asserted in accordance with sections 77 and 78 of the Copyright Design and Patent Act 1988.

Copyright © Roger Underwood 2021
For information contact via email: regorwoodunder@gmail.com

Published through Writers' Champion imprint of MAPublisher (Penzance)
Printed in UK

ISBN-13: 978-1-910499-70-2

Cover designed and inside images by Mayar Akash
Cover image is of a Roger Lowry's painting
Typeset in Times Roman

Paper printed on is FSC Certified, lead free, acid free, buffered paper made from wood-based pulp. Our paper meets the ISO 9706 standard for permanent paper. As such, paper will last several hundred years when stored.

Acknowledgement

My thanks to Mayar Akash and Lowenna Helena Otf Kaute for enabling me to publish this book. My wife Sue Underwood and my friend Paula Cronick for their help and encouragement. Roger Lowry for the cover artwork.

Content

Chapter 1

The sun is rising and another day begins. Jago is a Cornish fisherman who, along with his cousin Denzil, goes fishing most days on their boat, called the Acorn. She is thirty feet long and has a small forward wheelhouse, leaving a spacious afterdeck for catching fish. Jago and Denzil both treasure the Acorn and with their love and care she has become one of Newlyn's finest fishing boats. Jago and Denzil have owned the Acorn since they were young boys. Their fathers' were boat builders and they built the Acorn from one very special oak tree. This tree was no ordinary tree, it was very special, as it possessed strange mystical powers. This is the story of events that lead to the building of the Acorn. Many years ago there was a holy man who travelled from village to village, and county to county telling stories of God to anyone who would listen to him. One day whilst he was on his travels, he found himself walking across a place called Bodmin moor, when suddenly, out of the blue, he was caught in a tremendous thunderstorm. This was no ordinary storm, it was more like a hurricane, and the wind was so strong he could hardly stand. He looked around desperately for shelter but there was none to be found. There was nothing but moorland shrub and gorse in every direction, there was no shelter for him anywhere. He was very tired and hungry and felt he couldn't go on for much longer.

Although the thunder and lightning flashed and crashed around him he wasn't afraid, for he believed God wouldn't allow him to die in such a way, but he was now an old man and was feeling he couldn't go on any further. He didn't know what to do, so he just sat down on the wet, mossy grass and waited. He looked into his shoulder bag, feeling around for the last of his food, but all he had left was a crust of bread, which had turned to pulp from the driving rain.

He sat with his head between his hands and waited, waiting for what he wasn't sure. It was then he noticed there were lots of small mushrooms growing all around him, these would not have been his first choice of food, but he was very hungry and he began eating them. They were very small so he had to eat a lot of them, but they were better than no food at all. Suddenly there was a tremendous clap of thunder, so loud it made his body shake. It was much louder than anything he had ever heard before. He stood up in shock. In front of him now stood the biggest oak tree he had ever see, it seemed to be glowing all over in a hallow of light. At the base of the trunk was an intense bright light. Then he heard a voice, it came from within him, saying, "This is the tree of help and it will bear no seed except for one acorn." Although he heard the words clearly they came from inside his own mind. He stood looking at the huge tree in bewilderment, the glow began to disappear and the light at the base of the trunk grew dimmer. He walked closer towards the tree, he could see a wedge shaped opening at the base of the trunk. Underneath its' branches the wind and rain seemed to have stopped. Each of its' branches was so heavily laden with leaves that they had acted like a big umbrella, everything within its' perimeter was dry.

He walked in closer to the tree toward the base of the trunk where the bright light had been. He saw a hollow in the trunk and he peered inside. He could see it was all smooth and shinning, as if it had been polished,

8

revealing the grain of the wood. Carved around the insides of the hollow were crevices shaped like bowls, these bowls were full of wild fruit and nuts. The floor inside the hollow was covered with pliable brown leaves, looking soft and inviting, as if ready to be slept on. He began eating the fruits and nuts, until he had eaten all he could eat, he curled up on the dry leaves and fell into a deep sleep.

While he was sleeping God was placing thoughts in his head, he would only become aware of these thoughts later when he awoke. Many hours passed. When he woke he found himself lying on the wet grass out in the open, there was no sign of a tree anywhere. "Perhaps it was all a dream?" he thought, but he didn't see how it could have been, it all felt so real. Then a voice within him began saying, "You have not been dreaming my friend, for you the tree was real. This was the tree of help, which can be in many places at the same time, anywhere around the world. This tree that saved your life, will bear no seed except for one acorn."

The holy man picked up his bag and once again began his travels. For many years he continued to travel telling his stories of God and the tree that saved his life. Then one day something inside him made him feel he should to go back to Bodmin moor, back to the place where the tree had first appeared to him. When he arrived at the field there was now a large, round, flat stone, sat on top the stone was a single acorn. He recalled the words that had been spoken to him years earlier, "This tree will bear no seed except for one acorn."

This was when he realized this was to be his last task on this earth.

But how was he to know where to put the acorn? Who would need it most? He knew God must know the answers to these questions and he decided it would be better to leave him to decide. So with the acorn in his bag he was once again ready to set off on his travels. In which direction should he go? It was then he realised he was already walking. It appeared the decision had been made for him. He walked for days covering many miles. Early on the fifth morning he stopped in his tracks, he knew at this moment his time had come to depart this world and he fell to the ground dead, with a smile of contentment on his face. The holy man had played his part – for now! As he fell to the ground, the acorn rolled to the edge of his bag, almost falling out.

Chapter 2

He had been walking towards the south west coast of Cornwall. His journey ended about two miles from a small fishing village called Mousehole. Not far from the village was a small cottage belonging to a local fisherman called Nimrod, who lived there with his ageing parents. It was a small, pretty cottage that seemed to squat down in amongst a cluster of trees, as if it were taking shelter. Alongside the front garden were rows of wicker crab pots all neatly stacked ready and waiting for the time they would be put back into the sea. Along the other side of the garden was an old white, crusty picket fence, and hanging from it was a long length of fishing net that Nimrod had begun to repair, something Nimrod had done many times before. It had just broken daylight and the sounds of a family starting the day could be heard from inside the cottage. In turn each of the curtains were drawn letting in the early morning light.

The front door of the cottage opened and out came a strong, weathered looking young man. He was wearing a blue faded fishing smock and a woollen hat with lots of darns in it. Over his shoulder he had a bag with a pasty his mother had made for him for his lunch, along with a bottle of cold tea. As he walked up the garden path Nimrod would always turn back to wave to his Mother, whom he knew would be watching him leave from the front window. He set off towards Mousehole and the sea. As he walked down the lane, kicking stones along the way, he began wondering what fish he might catch that day, would it be the day his fortunes would change with a bumper catch. As he rounded the corner he looked toward one of the fields that lined the lane, he could see way over in the distance what looked like somebody lying on the ground at the far side of the field. He stopped and looked for a moment. He decided maybe he should go and take a look. As he grew nearer he could see it appeared to be a man. Nimrod went up closer toward him; asking, "Are you alright?" there was no reply. As he got closer he could see this man must have been some sort of priest or holy man as he was wearing a brown habit and he had a large wooden cross hanging from his neck. He spoke to him again and again but there was no answer. As he stood over the holy man he realised he was dead. He noticed the man, whoever he was, had died with a big smile on his face. Nimrod couldn't help but wonder what had pleased him so much as he died. Suddenly the reality of the moment hit Nimrod, what should he do? His first instinct was to run back home and tell his mother and father and let them decide what was best to do.

He ran back home as quickly as he could. His parents were startled at Nimrods sudden re- appearance and insisted he calm down and tell them what had happened. He was out of breath from running, and was gasping for air between the words as he tried to explain what he'd discovered. His parents found it all very hard to take in, but his father said he would get dressed and they should go back to the field where Nimrod had found this holy man.

They left the cottage and hurried back down the lane towards the field. When they arrived they came to a sudden halt. On the grass where the holy man had been laying was only the robe he'd been wearing, his wooden cross and the old bag he had been carrying. Father and son looked at each other in disbelief. What had happened? Where had the holy man gone? They exchanged various explanations but still had no answers.

Finally they decided they would take the robe, cross and bag to their local priest and see if he could help them to find the identity of the holy man. As Nimrod picked up the bag, the acorn that had been lying on the edge of it rolled out onto the grass. They started to walk back across the field and without noticing Nimrod stood on the acorn, pressing it into the ground. They set off for the village of Paul, which was on the hillside overlooking Mousehole, to find their local priest. Along the way to the village they discussed what could have happened, trying to find an explanation for this man's disappearance. It didn't take them long to reach the church and find the priest. Nimrod explained to the priest all that had taken place. The priest sat quietly listening to Nimrod's story. When he had finished telling the story the priest told them he had heard of a holy man who had roamed the countryside telling his stories of God and of a mystical oak tree. The description did seem to fit that of the man Nimrod had found in the field, but as to what became of his body would, for the moment have to remain a mystery. The priest agreed to keep the robe, cross and bag safely at the church.

The years passed and the story of the holy man was told over and over as they sat around the hearth on long winter evenings. Nimrod had grown into a mature man with a wife and two sons of his own. He still lived in the cottage he had shared with his parents who had died some years before. His sons were named Pirran, who was fourteen and Treeve who was thirteen. They were lively young boys and liked to be kept busy. So, on one wet and windy day, when Nimrod was unable to go to sea, he decided he would tell them the story of the holy man he had found in the field all those years before.

They listened hard to his every word in anticipation of what was to come next! When he finished telling them the story the boys pleaded with him to take them to the place where he had found the holy man. Nimrod told them it was far too wet and windy to be going out. But they would not be put off and kept on and on until finally Nimrod gave in and agreed to take them. It was still raining very hard so they put on their oilskins and wellies and made their way to the field. As they were leaving the boy's mother, Lowenna, called to them, "You two, make sure you stay out of the mud, I know what you are like." Closing the garden gate behind them Nimrod led the way. As they walked he told them it had been a long time since he had last walked along this particular lane and hoped he could remember in which field it had all happened. The boys were really excited and kept asking if they nearly there. "It's not far now" replied Nimrod. As they rounded the next bend Nimrod knew this was the field. They walked into it, Nimrod stopped for a moment, he was looking very puzzled, the boys asked him what was wrong, " Well", he answered, "just over there," he pointed into the distance "right over there, on far side of the field, right there where that big tree is, is the very spot I found the holy man." They walked up closer to the tree. Nimrod found it hard to believe what he was seeing, it was an enormous oak tree.

He explained to the boys how an oak tree of that size would take a very long time to grow and to reach this size would take about two hundred

14

years! They were all stood under the tree looking up through its magnificent branches. Even though the wind and rain were still blowing strong its branches hardly seemed to move. The boys were speechless and stood in awe of the tree. They reached and touched the trees crusty bark, it seemed to give a sense of strength and reliability and gave them all a tingly feeling inside. Pirran broke the silence, saying "Could this be the tree the holy man spoke of?" Nimrod nodded his head, "I don't know." He fell silent, in deep thought as he recalled the story the priest had told him all those years before when he had taken the holy man's belongings to him at the church. Then, thinking aloud, he said; "It must be true?" Seeing their father like this was making the boys feel a little uneasy. Nimrod held out his hands to the boys and gestured it was time for them to go back home.

The boys glanced at each other nervously but understood their father knew best and they each took his hands and turned to walk away. As they walked away the boys looked to their father for reassurance that everything would be all right. Nimrod was feeling confused and bewildered about what part he and his family were to play in the fate of this tree. He knew deep down inside, he or someone in his family was destined to play a part in whatever was to come. What bothered him most was, how was he to know who and when it might happen? He pondered on these questions. They had walked on about fifty yards or so away from the tree, when all three of them felt an overwhelming compulsion to turn around and look back toward the tree. As they turned and looked back they all saw a figure of a man dressed in a long brown robe, standing under the tree. The boys moved in closer to their father and he wrapped his arms around them protectively.

The figure under the tree slowly raised his arm and spoke to them; "Please don't be afraid, I am only a messenger. Don't you recognise me young fisherman?" Nimrod did, it all came back clearly, it was the holy man he had found all those years before. He was stunned and wondered what was coming next. The holy man spoke again, even though he was some distance away his voice was clear and they could hear his every word, as if he were stood next to them. He said, "All the events that have taken place were destiny and were meant to be. As I was once, you and your sons are now part of the future. Things will present themselves in the way they are meant to be. Remember, there is no grief in destiny and love is never lost. Go about your life as you would have done and in time all will be revealed."

As he finished speaking he raised both his arms and slowly faded away until he had totally disappeared. Being so young the boys didn't understand what they had seen and heard, they turned to their father for an explanation, but he wasn't sure himself and told them he felt all that had taken place that day and the events of the past must be for a purpose. He thought it would be best for the time being if they didn't tell anyone about what had happened. They should do as the holy man had told them and one day they would understand the full meaning of all the things they'd seen and heard.

Chapter 3

Many years had passed and the brothers were now young men. Pirran was tall and broad across the shoulders; he had sandy hair and a ruddy complexion. Treeve was smaller with mousey hair and paler complexion; he looked like his mother and had her kindly temperament. Even though the brothers had such different personalities they got on very well, they seemed to complement one another in many different ways and it seemed only natural they should work together. As boys they had spent many hours with their father helping him with repairs and maintenance on his boat. It was working with the wood that interested them the most. So when it came time to leave school they were both apprenticed to a local boat repairers in Newlyn harbour, in a long established business called Seaks. It was hard for them at first, the hours were long and their apprentices' pay wasn't very much. As the years passed they grew more skilful and they enjoyed their work very much. When their apprenticeships ended the owner of the boatyard told the boys he would only be able to keep on one of them. They were both as good as each other at their job so he was going to leave the choice to them which one of them would stay. This came as a blow to them as they had always thought of themselves as a pair. They talked at great length, trying to decide what to do, neither wanted to stay on at Seaks without the other.

They went home that night and spoke to their parents about their situation and asked for their advice. Their father sat thinking for a moment then he asked them how much money they had saved up. Both Treeve and Pirran had been very thrifty with their money over the years and between them they had managed to save a fair amount money. "That's it then" said Nimrod, "You both leave Seaks, you buy more heavy tools and start your own business." The boys thought for a moment, then looked at each other, smiled and began laughing with excitement. Yes, this is what they would do! This was how they began. Now they have a thriving business and a reputation for good work. They have a small boatshed in Mousehole, near the slipway in the village, where they had spent their childhoods. They were now both married, Treeve to Karenza and Pirran to Tegan each of them had moved into new homes overlooking the harbour in Newlyn. Like themselves their wives had always been good friends as children and they all went everywhere together.

Newlyn was a much larger village than Mousehole. It had a very busy fishing port and there were several hundred boats using the harbour. During the winter months most of the boats from Mousehole would travel to Newlyn to take shelter from the storms that regularly raged during the winter months.

The entrance to Mousehole harbour was sealed off each winter to protect the harbour and the village from the winter seas. To do this they used large baulks of timber placed across the harbour entrance making a barrier between the rough sea and the calm water inside the harbour. In years gone by the houses on the quayside were regularly flooded by the winter gales as the waves crashed in through the harbour entrance. Now with the harbour modifications in place winter had become a much quieter in Mousehole.

18

Only the sound of the sea crashing against the wooden baulks could be heard during the storms.

Treeve and Pirran's father, Nimrod, was now an old man. He had retired from fishing and now spent most of his spare time at the boatshed with Treeve and Pirran helping them when and where they needed him. The boatshed was near the top of the old slipway in Mousehole. It was once a very busy building, it was used by many of the old luggers. In the days when herring fishing was the main income for the fishermen, their nets would be stored and repaired there. It was also where they would make the preservative for their fishing nets. This concoction was made from either a mixture of oak bark or birch bark which was put on the nets to help preserve them from the salty environment they would be in most of the time. It was a very old building, built of granite, like most of the cottages in the village. It was thought to be at least two hundred years old and by the look of the roof, it looked like it. The weight of scantle stone and the cement wash on top of it made its' roof trusses sag and bend into very strange shapes. The boys had planned to replace the roof when they had some free time, but as the time passed they always seemed to be too busy to be able to do it.

Inside the building it was all carefully planned out. The centre area was left clear for whatever boat they were working on at the time, along one side were racks of sawn timbers of assorted sizes. This timber planking had to be stacked and aired with great care, making sure they were all straight and true preventing them from warping as they dried.

On the other side of the shed were rows of shelves and boxes where all the specialised tools were kept. Each of them having its own special place, Nimrod would spend most of his time cleaning and replacing the tools after they had been used. This was a very important job, there were so many tools and they were so expensive it was important to keep them safe and in good order. Of course it also helped the boys save time when they were working if they didn't have to search for their tools!

The old man enjoyed working with his sons at the boatyard. He had his own special chair in the top right hand corner of the boatshed, next to the old log stove. He could warm himself and light his pipe while he contemplated all he could see and what he could see made him very happy. From his chair he could look down through the boatshed, he could see the whole of Mousehole harbour and out onto the sea. He watched the coming and going of all his old friends, reflecting on the times he had spent with them out at sea on his own boat. He dearly missed his boat and the freedom he felt when he was out on the sea. He didn't have the health he used to have, his old bones ached with the cold so he had to resign himself to playing his part on shore. It was his work in the boatshed that kept him going, plus the occasional yarns he would share with his older fishermen friends who would stop by the boatshed.

He would sit in his chair on warm sunny days and reflect on how lucky he'd been throughout his life. He wondered what kind of life he might have had if he had not come upon the holy man when he was young and fit. All through his life the holy man had never been far from his thoughts. There had been many times during his life when he had to make important decisions at sea and he had always felt there had been someone helping him

20

make the right choices. Many times he had been back to the oak tree, he would sit under the tree looking up through its' powerful branches and watch the leaves gracefully dancing in the breeze.

Always the words he had heard back along would come to him. It was as if the tree telling him not to forget. Often he would sit with Treeve and Pirran around the old stove in the boatshed after their work was done. They would talk and remember together the things the holy man had said. Nimrod could not help thinking, as he was getting older, that this destiny the holy man spoke of must be for one of his sons and not for him. Still he hoped to see the outcome before he died. Treeve and Pirran could not remember as well as their father and they were always asking him questions about it, endlessly looking for a logical explanation for the events they had witnessed as children. Being so young at the time they had not been unable to fully comprehend the wisdom they had heard that day. Their memories of what had happened were beginning to fade and they hoped by talking to their father would help them remember and understand better.

Chapter 4

Treeve and Pirran each have a son of their own. As with most other things in their lives, they married and became fathers at more or less at the same time. Pirran named his son Jago and Treeve named his son Denzil. These two boys were growing up very close to each other, just as their fathers had done. Especially as they lived so near to each other, spending time in each other's homes. They had become as inseparable as their fathers had been as boys. Denzil was tall for his age; he had fair hair and an impish grin that seemed to be permanently on his face! Jago was shorter with sandy hair; he was more thick set and strong looking, although he was the quieter of the two boys. As they were now six years old and better able to understand about wandering off and getting into mischief, their dads used to take them with them to Mousehole and the boatshed. It was only at weekends and in the school holidays but the boys loved it and looked forward to going there. If the tide was out they would play on the beach where the small punts were tied up. They would sit in the dinghies pretending to be on the open sea catching mackerel. They would tie a seagull feather to a piece of string and jig it up and down, just pretending, it was lovely to see them so happy!

Grandfather Nimrod loved to watch them from his chair in the boatshed, he often thought how he would like to sneak up on them one day and when they weren't looking tie a real mackerel to their piece of string. That would make them jump for joy! What a happy place to live.

It had been a good summer, the weather had been fine, the cobbled streets had seen a lot of tourists, which meant all the shopkeepers were very happy. The fishermen were pleased, the mackerel fishing had been good, the shoals of fish came in close to shore and they were big enough for everyone to share, everybody was happy. The sand on Mousehole's beach had seen more than its fair share of holiday makers enjoying Cornwall's glorious summer weather and all would be looking forward to the next years holiday season after the winter surf had once again pound it's golden granules back into its winter neatness ready for the following year.

Autumn had arrived and Mousehole and the village was beginning to yawn. The seasonal gift shops had put up the shutters. The fishermen had taken their boats around to Newlyn harbour ready for winter shelter. The locals of Mousehole had begun to prepare the timber baulks to be put back into place across the harbour entrance to protect them once again from the winter seas. Treeve and Pirran had their busiest time coming up. Most fishermen and yachtsmen take advantage of the winter months, to have their repairs done. Throughout the summer the fishing boats have been working hard and most of them would have had minor damage or would just take this time for basic maintenance. Most of the smaller local boats would either be craned out onto the quay at Penzance or put up onto the slipway at Newlyn.

Treeve and Pirran were kept busy travelling with their boat repairs. They travelled from harbour to harbour along the coast from Porthleven to Sennen cove, repairing and preparing the boats for the coming spring so they are ready for work when the weather breaks. By November Mousehole is well prepared for the coming winter. The harbour has been sealed off and most of the boats have been taken around to the safety of Newlyn. The tourists have all gone home and the village has slipped into a sleep, all except the seagulls, they are always awake! They are constantly squawking as if they are all in a permanent disagreement with each other. They line the rooftops and the quay walls constantly scanning the area for some distance morsel that might be coming their way. If one seagull spots something, he will let the rest of them know and before you know it, they will all be heading for it.

An unbelievable noise will break out as every gull in the area will sweep down on it, each hoping to be the first there! They are not capable of keeping a secret! Today the seagulls are unusually quiet as they line the rooftops. The smoke from the chimneys of the village was quietly spiralling above them in the gentle breeze, but that was about to change! The seagulls are always first to know when a storm is on its way. On the horizon is a faint purple tinge can be seen, a sign that a storm was on its way. The local people know the signs; a few old fishermen were already on the quay wall surveying the sea and its mood. It wasn't looking good, the swell and the surf was building momentum. The wind had turned and picked up in strength it was blowing on shore, the clouds on the horizon were getting darker, slowly but surely a storm was on its way. Just in front of the clouds were the mackerel boats heading back, running for shelter at Newlyn Harbour, their engines were working hard pushing against the sea. The smoke from the cottage chimneys was forming a definite direction in the ever freshening wind. The rows of seagulls just sat observing, their heads tucked into their bodies but leaving one eye still looking on. Each of the birds was in its' own special

24

place, waiting to ride out the storm that was certain to arrive soon. The storm was now at its' worst, the wind was whistling up through the cobbled streets, the rain was fierce, it sounded like small pebbles crashing against the windows panes. There was nobody to be seen on the streets. This night was to be one of the worst storms the people of Mousehole had seen for a long time. There was surely going to be plenty of damage along the coast before this storm was over. All through the night the storm raged, rattling doors and hooting back drafts down chimney pipes. As dawn broke the storm eased. The clouds began to break up and the rain stopped as if someone had turned off a tap.

It was about nine o'clock next morning when Treeve and Pirran arrived at the boatshed, to their horror they found it no longer had a roof! All that was left were broken timbers. All the scantle stones that used to be on the roof were scattered in every direction, it looked like a bomb had hit it! By now the wind had almost gone, the sun was shining and the sea had calmed down. If all the debris had not been in front of them they wouldn't have believed there had been any storm at all.

A crowd of villagers was beginning to gather around the boatshed. When something like this strikes in Cornwall there is never any shortage of helping hands. People on the Cornish coast are a very closely-knit and well known for their generosity when it comes to giving a helping hand when somebody needs help. They know next time it may well be them in trouble. Somebody was missing this morning. Treeve turned to his brother, "Where is father? He is usually at the boatyard long before us." "Has anyone seen my father?" shouted Treeve, but no one in the crowd had seen him.

Immediately both knew something was wrong. Treeve and Pirran quickly made their way to their father's house. When they arrived they could see the curtains were still drawn, now they knew for sure something was wrong! Pirran banged on the front door while Treeve went around to the back. Pirran was still knocking the front door when it opened. It was Treeve, he had climbed through an open window. They rushed upstairs to their father's room. He was in bed. He laid so still, no movement at all. They stood at the edge of the room, each waiting for the other to move or say something. Treeve walked over to the bed and Pirran followed. He lifted his father's hand to feel for a pulse. Still holding his hand he turned to Pirran and in a trembling voice said, "I can't feel any pulse, I think father is dead Pirran!"

They both sank to the floor and sobbed as they leaned against their father's bed. Then Treeve noticed something in his father's clenched fist. It looked like a piece of paper. He gently pulled it through Nimrods fingers and smoothed out the crumpled paper. It had four words written on it; "The tree is down." They looked at each other, both with tears running down their faces. What could it mean? They looked at their father, he had a happy expression on his face, as if content in the knowledge of something the boys were yet to find out. His part had been played; he had cast the die and was now content. Treeve remembered the words of the holy man; "There is no grief in destiny, love is never lost."

Just then there was a knock at the front door. Pirran went down to see who it was. He opened the door to a man he didn't know. The man asked to speak to either Treeve or Pirran. "I'm Pirran, can I help you?" "I'm from Hobbs Farm, a couple of miles away," said the man. "I was told to come and speak to you to find out where you wanted the tree taken." "Which tree?" asked Treeve, looking puzzled? "The oak tree that blew down last night on my land" Immediately the significance of the note in their fathers' hand became clear.

"Who told you to come here to see us?" "I really couldn't say who he was," replied the farmer, "I have never seen him before. About 10'o'clock last night there was a knock on my door and this old man stood there. He told me that the oak tree in my field had blown down. He asked me if I would sell it to him. I asked him what he wanted it for; he told me the timber would be used to build a boat. Well, I had no use for it, and as he offered me such a good price, I said he could have it, so it was agreed. He gave me this address and told me to be there at exactly 11'o'clock this morning and to ask for either Treeve or Pirran, so here I am."

Pirran called his brother to explain to him what was happening. Treeve asked the farmer could he describe what this man looked like. "Well," said the farmer "he reminded me of a monk, he had a long brown robe and a bag hanging from his shoulder, he had a small wooden cross around his neck. Do you recognise him?" "Oh yes we do!" said both, Treeve and Pirran. "I'll tell you one thing I found very strange," said the farmer, "when I opened the door to this man, the storm was raging and raining very hard, yet I noticed his garment didn't seem to be getting wet. The rose bushes either side of the doorway were swaying and dancing in the wind but the man's long hair remained undisturbed." The boys knew their father must have been aware of all this, that is why he looked so happy as he lay on his bed. Although he would be sorely missed by his sons they knew he was happy knowing the destiny of the tree. Now it was time for Treeve and Pirran to play their part.

Chapter 5

Four years passed, the new roof was on the boatshed and Nimrod had been laid to rest in the village churchyard. It was high on the hillside and overlooked the village where he had been born and spent most of his life. He had always told the boys when his time came this was where he wanted to be, overlooking the sea and the village he loved. The whole village turned out for his funeral. He was well liked by many people who wanted to pay their last respects. The small church was full and the people spilled over into the churchyard. There were many tears shed that day.

Treeve and Pirran had the tree taken to the sawmill at Newlyn. It was the finest timber they had ever seen. There was more than enough to build a strong little boat and repair the roof of the boatshed. Once again the friendship of the local people helped them to rebuild the roof. Anyone who was able turned up to offer help. All the scantle stones from the original roof were carefully and painstakingly secured onto the strong new timbers. When it was finished it was a fine job. At first the boatshed looked odd with a clean straight line along the centre of the roof, the old sagging roof that had been there for so long was gone. Everyone that had helped in the repair could be well satisfied with a good job. With the new strong oak timbers Treeve and Pirran felt sure it would last another hundred years.

To show their gratitude for all the help they decided to give everyone a treat. They had arranged with the landlord of the Blue Dolphin Inn at Newlyn, to lay out a large supper for as many as he could feed.

Everyone was invited and a great deal of food and ale was consumed! Treeve and Pirran thanked everyone who had helped with the roof and given them support when their father died. They then suggested everyone have some fun. The Blue Dolphin Inn was a happy place that day and all had a wonderful time exchanging memories of good old Nimrod.

The new boat was now nearing completion in the boatshed. It was surely the best boat they'd ever built. Both Treeve and Pirran had put in many hours work, and now it was almost finished. Standing back to look and admire their handy work. "Lovely," said Treeve "I think we can be pleased with that." This was a special moment for the brothers. They were very satisfied with what they had accomplished, but there was somebody missing, and they wished he could have been there with them to share this moment, all together.

The brothers were very pleased with what they had built, all that remained was to add a few finishing touches and fit the engine. The timber planking had been lovingly sanded and smoothed, it had received many coats of the finest varnish, and was shining like a piece of glass. The waterline was painted with white gloss paint and the bottom was painted with bright red anti- foul paint to protect it from the seawater. The new bronze, three-blade propeller gleamed like a yellow diamond, looking eager to thrash it's way through the water. Yes, this surely was a special boat. The brothers decided they would work into the night to install the engine. It was a brand new diesel engine, the very best; it was painted bright blue and looked ready for plenty of work.

They put rope slings about it and slowly winched it out of its' wooden packing case. Gently they moved it into position ready to lower it into the boat, where strong oak engine beds were waiting to receive it. The ratchet on the pulley clicked away and the engine slowly lowered into its' new home. Treeve was inside the boat ready to bolt down the engine with four big stainless steel bolts, these would keep the engine securely in place. He signalled to Pirran it was in position and to stop the winch. Treeve quickly slipped the bolts down into the holes and the engine was secured. All that remained was for them to connect the main shaft to the gearbox, connect the fuel supply from the tank and finally connect the electrical system to the ignition.

By three 'o'clock in the morning all was finished. It really was a magnificent looking boat and the brothers were well satisfied with their work, Nimrod would have been so proud of them. They made their way home for a well-deserved rest. On the way Treeve asked his brother what he thought they should do with the boat now it was finished, "After all," he said " we're not fishermen we're boat builders." "I don't know," replied Pirran, " I suppose we shall just have to wait and see what presents itself."

Later that week the whole family went to the boatshed for the first starting of the engine. Treeve, his wife Karenza and their son Denzil, now ten years old. Pirran, his wife Tegan and their son Jago also ten years old. Treeve and Pirran had decided a long time ago not to tell their wives or Denzil and Jago what had happened to them all those years ago. Mainly because it was difficult to explain, especially when they weren't all that sure about it themselves. They all stood in front of the boatshed as Treeve opened the

31

main door and the light shone in. It looked splendid as the sunlight shone in all around it. The light seemed to darken the rest of the boatshed with its' brilliance. The varnish and paintwork radiated brightly. "Yes, this is certainly a special boat." said Treeve quietly to Pirran, who nodded, smiling in agreement.

Jago and Denzil broke the silence by running up through the boatshed toward the ladder that was up against the side of the boat. Up the ladder they went and onto the boat, quickly followed by their parents. Karenza said to Treeve, "I must admit it's a lovely looking boat." "Yes," agreed Tegan, "you should get a good price for this one." "No," said Treeve, "we're not selling it." "Well, what are you going to do with it then?" she asked. "It's for the boys." he answered. "Yes," added Pirran, "it's for our boys." Everybody just looked at each other in amazement and nobody was more puzzled than Treeve and Pirran themselves. They hadn't a clue why they had said it was for the boys! "For the boys?" said Karenza," but they're only ten years old, they won't be able to use it for years." " Yes, we know that," said Pirran," but we thought we could go with them on weekends and do the odd bit of mackerel fishing."

The boys couldn't believe their ears! "It's for us!" said Jago to Denzil. They must have been the happiest boys in Cornwall at that moment. "Well," said Tegan," I'm not in disagreement with you. I think it's a good idea that they have something to look forward to when they're older. But you must make sure they never take the boat out alone." Denzil and Jago were over the moon, the boat was actually going to be theirs'! "When is it going to be launched?" Denzil asked his father. "Before she can be put into the water she will have to be named," said Pirran "you boys will have to decide what she is going to be called, have you any ideas?" They thought for a moment but nothing immediately came to mind. Tegan suggested that the boys each have a piece of paper and they should write down their choice. Then the pieces of paper be put into a box and Pirran would draw one out. Whatever was written on that piece of paper would be the name of the boat. They all agreed. They each wrote a name on their piece of paper, and then they folded them and put them in the box. Treeve held the box while Pirran reached in and picked out a piece of paper. He unfolded it and read out what was written; "The Acorn," he said quietly to Treeve. He showed the paper to him and they both agreed it was a good name. "Yes, a very appropriate name for this boat." said Treeve. "Come on, hurry up, whose name is it?" urged Denzil. You could see the excitement in their faces; if they had to wait much longer they would burst! "Alright," said Treeve, "which one of you wrote The Acorn?" "I did!" shouted Denzil. "No, it was me." added Jago. "Come on now you both couldn't have written the same name." said Karenza. "But I did." protested Jago. "I wrote The Acorn on my piece of paper." "So did I" insisted Denzil. "Wait now" said Treeve. He took the other piece of paper from the box, unfolded it and sure enough the words The Acorn were written on it! He held up the two pieces of paper for everyone to see. Karenza and Tegan were amazed. The odds must be a million to one something like this would happen, but the brothers knew differently.

They needn't have worried about what to do, they knew for sure the course they were on was the right one, and the holy man had played a part this day. The boat now had a name and new owners; all that remained was to turn the key in the ignition. Treeve suggested as Denzil and Jago were joint owners they should both hold the key and start the engine together. This was a very exciting moment for the two ten year-old boys. A day they will probably never forget. They took their position in the wheelhouse, both nervously holding the key. "We will count to three, then you both turn the key until the engine starts." said Treeve. "Are you ready? One, two, three." The engine chugged slowly, it picked up speed until the revs were right and the engine ticked over like a precision watch. Light grey smoke shimmered out through the exhaust pipe in the transom of the boat. The timbers vibrated because she was high and dry on her blocks. The ladder on the side of the boat was dancing around in sympathy with the vibrating timbers.

Karenza and Tegan were showing signs of nervousness; they wanted to get back down on solid ground before the boat made it's own way into the sea! "Time to check the gears." said Treeve. He pushed the gear lever into the ahead position, with a clunk the shaft threw itself into motion. The propeller could be heard humming like a bee. The shaft was turning on it's bearings to perfection. "Now for reverse gear," said Treeve. He pulled the gear lever into neutral and then into reverse. Again the shaft whizzed back turning in the opposite direction. "Perfection!" said Pirran " The shaft is straight and true and turning like a dream." Treeve reached for the stop button on the control panel. "It's time we stopped her or else she will over heat with no water running through the engine to cool it."

Karenza and Tegan were very relieved when the engine stopped and speedily made their way down the ladder. All the 'men' aboard had a good laugh while Treeve helped the ladies down the ladder. Once back on solid

34

ground, Tegan said; "As much as I like the boat, I would rather be on the ground." "Next week, "said Treeve "the tides will be high and it will be a good time to launch the boat, We will christen her in style and pour a bottle of champagne on her bows" "That's a good idea, " agreed Pirran " are you two boys in agreement with this?" As if he needed to ask! "Fantastic!" they yelled. Denzil was at the wheel and Jago was at the gear controls, imagining themselves at sea already! Tegan turned to Karenza and said; "I know two boys that won't be doing much sleeping tonight." Treeve and Pirran laughed. Denzil and Jago didn't even hear what was said, they were too busy sailing across the ocean!

Throughout the next week Treeve and Pirran spent most of the time preparing log rollers on the slipway. All the pulley blocks and ropes were in place. All was ready to pull the boat down onto the log rollers, all being well she would gently slip into the sea. Pirran had painted her name across the stern of the boat in gold and white paint. When they saw the name in place they realised no other name could have looked so right. The launch was scheduled for Saturday at ten 'o'clock in the morning. It was to be the highest tide of the year and perfect for launching the boat. Most of the village people knew when the launch was and would most certainly be there to give a helping hand where needed. The launching of a new boat in Mousehole is always a special occasion, but for Treeve and Pirran this was to be a particularly special day.

Saturday morning came and there was already a crowd gathering at the boatshed when they arrived. Everyone greeted Treeve and Pirran and wished them luck. Treeve opened the doors, they all gathered to the front of the doorway for a glimpse of the boat. The doors swung open, and the boat came into view. There was a loud cheer and everyone clapped in appreciation of the beautiful boat in front of them. Treeve and Pirran felt very proud, for more reasons than anybody else but themselves could know. Meanwhile Denzil and Jago were very busy telling everyone gathered that it was going to be their boat, and very soon they would be able to take her out by themselves. Treeve and Pirran, with some of the locals, had gone into the shed to make final preparations; who was to hold which rope, who was to push and who was to pull etc. Everything was ready all that was left to do was to hit the two wooden wedges from under the keel and the boat should roll forward until the ropes tightened. "Is everyone ready, holding their ropes?" asked Pirran. Everyone nodded. Treeve and Pirran, each with a large sledge hammer hit out the wooden wedges. The boat suddenly came to life as the wedges moved away from under her keel. With a creek and groan she started to move forward on her blocks, the ropes snapped tight with a twang.

It was time to christen her before she moved onto the sea. Treeve called for Karenza and Tegan to bring the bottle of champagne. It is a long tradition in Cornwall that only a woman can christen a boat. Throughout a boat's life, no matter what part of the world it may be it will always be female and be called 'she'. Pirran climbed the ladder with a length of string tied to the neck of the champagne bottle. He passed the bottle to Tegan and Karenza so that they could name the boat together. He secured the other end of the string to a cleat on the deck. Everything was quiet; Tegan and Karenza said the words they had rehearsed all week; "God bless the Acorn and all who sail on her." They swung the bottle towards the boat and it smashed into

36

the stem post. The boat was now well and truly christened! Everybody clapped and cheered, by now the crowd had doubled and they made a tremendous noise. It was a fantastic atmosphere.

The water was in sight, the tide was fully in. The excitement was almost too much for Denzil and Jago; they were jumping up and down, clapping their hands, giggling and chuckling, running back and forth to make sure they didn't miss the boat coming down the slipway. Slowly the boat inched its' way down towards the water. The ropes stretched tight and the pulley blocks creaked with the weight of their load. As the log rollers were leaving the stern of the boat, two of the locals were quickly picking them up and running to the front, replacing them ready for the boat to pass over them again. The water lapped the front of the boat, her first taste of the sea. She was ready for the sea and could now be left to finish the journey alone. Treeve just left two ropes attached to stop her drifting away when she hit the water, he held one at the stern and Pirran had attached one to the bow. Everyone else had slackened their ropes and were ready.

Treeve shouted to the crowd to stand back and he began the countdown from ten to zero. Everyone joined in, Denzil and Jago could be heard clearly above the crowd as they shouted as loud as they could. As zero approached the noise increased, a huge cheer went up as they shouted zero. Treeve let go his rope and down she went sliding into the sea! Denzil and Jago were leaping about with excitement. The two ropes still attached, snapped tight and the boat came to a halt. She bobbed up and down as she sat on the clear blue sea. She had come to life; she was where she was meant to be. The brothers pulled her back to the side of the slipway; there everyone was jostling for their first glance into the new boat. Treeve and Pirran tied new red and white fenders to her side to stop her getting scratched against the side of the slipway.

Denzil and Jago wasted no time they were first on board, after all they were the proud owners! Treeve and Pirran thanked all their friends who had helped them with the launch and suggested a celebration at the Blue Dolphin Inn. This idea was well received and everyone started to make off in this direction. Treeve called the boys and told them where they were going. There was no way they were going to leave the boat just yet. After consulting Pirran, he told them they could stay for a while longer. The water alongside the slipway wasn't very deep and soon the tide would be out, leaving the boat high and dry, so the brothers left their sons to it.

Already Denzil and Jago had found some old rags and were busy polishing the brass work, just as any proud new owner would have done! Although only ten years old, both boys had a good knowledge of boats, boats had been a large part of their lives. They were very proficient in all fishing and nautical terms. Now they were on their own, all the grownups out of the way, they really felt masters of their own vessel. As they were busying themselves around the boat Denzil looked up to see a strange man standing on the slipway looking down on them. "It's a fine strong boat," the man said. "The best," agreed Denzil, "The best in all of Cornwall." "I'm glad to see it's in the right hands." said the man. "What do you mean?" asked Jago. The man smiled and said; "One day you will know, until then look after your boat well. I have to go now but one day we will see each other again." The man, who was wearing a brown robe, smiled and walked away. The boys didn't

38

pay much attention to the man they just carried on with their work on the boat.

A few hours later Treeve and Pirran returned from the Blue Dolphin. The boys were still on board desperately looking for something to polish. They had cleaned everything on board, but were busy checking just in case they had missed something! "Come on you two." said Treeve "it's time to go home now, tomorrow you can have your first ride on her." "Fantastic!!" was the reply "Where will we go?" "We'll just take her out for a test run to make sure everything is working properly. If it all goes well we'll take her out next weekend and do some fishing." said Pirran. Treeve went up to the boatshed, swept up the broken glass, put all the ropes away and locked the doors. Meanwhile Pirran and the boys were double checking the ropes on the boat making sure they were secure. They were tied onto old iron rings on the slipway. When they were certain she was safe for the night they made their way home to Newlyn. The boys did nothing else but talk about their wonderful boat all the way home. They were so excited about tomorrows trip they could hardly wait for the next day to arrive!

Chapter 6

They were all up early next morning. The two boys were making sure they weren't left behind, by getting up at the crack of dawn. They pestered their dads to get up, they were so impatient to get to the boat. It was around nine 'o'clock when they finally arrived at the Acorn. The two boys ran on ahead and were waiting for what seemed a lifetime for their fathers to join them. The tide was just starting to lap around the boat and by the time they had set up the sail on the mizzen mast the boat was just beginning to float. Pirran told the boys to each put on their lifejackets. "You can never be too careful at sea." said, Treeve "I think we're just about ready to cast off now." said Pirran.

The two boys went into the cabin and waited anxiously. Pirran untied the forward rope and Treeve pulled the rope through the mooring ring at the stern. He went into the cabin ready to start the engine. One click of the key and she burst into life. Pirran quickly jumped on board, Treeve pushed the gear lever into forward and the boat slowly moved away from the slipway. When they were a safe distance away, Treeve turned the wheel to starboard and pushed the throttle lever forward. "Right boys," said Pirran "here's the wheel, she's yours now, you can take her out of the harbour yourselves, you can each take a turn on the wheel." As Jago was nearest he had the first turn, after about ten minutes it was Denzil's turn. Pirran and Treeve stood back and watched them, they were two extremely happy boys. Pirran turned to Treeve and said, "I think it's about time we opened up the throttle, let's see what speed she can do." "Yes," replied Treeve, he shouted to Denzil to press the throttle further forward, "Don't press it down too fast, take it gently" advised Treeve.

The boat immediately responded by rising up at the bow and digging in at the stern leaving a large white turbulent wake behind it. The speedometer on the dash was reading a speed of seven knots and still rising. The spray was splashing over her bows as she ploughed her way through the waves. The boy's faces were beaming with delight as the water sprayed up and over onto the wheelhouse windows. The boat had reached a speed of eight and a half knots and seemed to holding steady at that. "Not a bad speed for a boat of this type" said Pirran, Treeve agreed, he was very pleased with it's performance and he knew she was going to be an excellent sea boat. Denzil and Jago were in their element, round and round in circles they went, they were having so much fun, they had forgotten their fathers were there with them, they were having such a good time!

Treeve and Pirran had decided Newlyn would the best place to keep the boat, they could use Nimrods' old mooring, this was in deeper water, but still inside the safety of the harbour, but more importantly by being on this mooring they wouldn't have to wait for the tide to come in and out when they wanted to use the boat, it would always be ready to use at any time. Nimrod would have been very proud if he could have seen this beautiful boat out on the open sea, especially as it was made from a very special tree that meant so much to him. Pirran shouted to Denzil, who was at the wheel, it was time for them to head toward Newlyn harbour. He told them they would be keeping

41

the Acorn on their grandfathers' old mooring. "Fantastic!" said the boys. "We'll be able to see it from our bedroom windows. It will be so close to home we'll be able to go to the boat straight from school." Treeve and Pirran laughed. "Well," said Treeve "If they can see the boat from the house, it means Karenza and Tegan will see it as well so they will be able to keep an eye on them!"

Every afternoon after school the boys would rush straight down to the boat. They had to row across the harbour to the mooring and to do this they used grandfathers' old dingy. This presented no problem, as they were both proficient at rowing dingys and they were both under strict instructions to have their life jackets on. Both knew their mothers would be keeping a close eye on them from their windows even though they were good swimmers for their age. Local schools placed a high priority on swimming lessons, as most of the population lived near the waters' edge, so all children were taught to swim at an early age. The boys would stay on the boat for about two hours, and then go home for their tea; heaven knows what they found to occupy themselves with for so long! If they washed the boat any more they would wash it away! Karenza and Tegan had an arrangement with the boys, when they saw their bedroom curtains drawn it was time to come home for tea. This seemed to work quite well, although most of the time the boys would still be half an hour late! They were becoming proper little Captains, breakfast, dinner and tea all they could talk about was the boat.

The weekend arrived and they were all up at the crack of dawn. This weekend was going to be their first trip out with the main mackerel fleet. The boys were very excited and looking forward to this; when they arrived at the harbour it was beginning to come alive as all the boats were starting up their engines and getting ready to leave. There were about sixty to seventy boats in the mackerel fleet all tied up alongside of each other in long tiers along the harbour walls. There averaged ten boats to each tier and one by one they cast off their ropes and made their way through the harbour entrance, forming a long chain of boats. When they were about a mile out to sea they split up into packs. Some went east of the bay; some went west of the bay. You could never be sure exactly where the mackerel would be each day. To make it easier to find them the first pack to find the fish would call to the others to join them.

Treeve and Pirran cast off the mooring ropes and the Acorn joined the other boats leaving the harbour. Now Denzil and Jago felt like real fishermen, they looked the part in their new yellow oilskins! They had come a mile from shore and had to decide which way to go, east or west. Treeve and Pirran decided they would try to the west, towards Lands End so they told Denzil to steer to starboard. Whilst the boys were at the wheel their fathers prepared the mackerel feathers, ready to start fishing. After a few miles of travelling along the coast they could see some of the boats ahead of them had stopped and seemed to be hauling fish into their boats. "Look they're pulling up mackerel, they've found the fish," said Pirran. Sure enough as they approached closer they could see mackerel, coming out of the sea like strings of silver dollars.

Treeve eased up on the throttle and pulled gear lever into the neutral position. The Acorn was now amongst thirty other boats, each of them about ten feet apart from one another. Treeve passed around the handlines, each

43

line had twenty mackerel feathers on it, and these were called sets. Each of the lines had a large lead weight attached to the end which would take the feathers quickly down into the sea. "You boys fish from the starboard side and we will fish the port side." said Treeve. He reminded them to be very careful as they shook the mackerel off the hooks and never to do it without wearing rubber gloves. "It will be very painful if you get one of them stuck in your hand." "Don't worry," assured Denzil "we will be very careful." Jago had his line ready first but waited for Denzil so they could start together and see who caught the first fish! Once Denzil was ready they dropped their lines down into the sea. No sooner had the lines dropped into the water they started to jerk and sag with the weight of mackerel on them, each fish trying to swim in a different direction. "I've got them!" shouted Denzil "So have I! " shouted Jago, laughing with excitement. They quickly began pulling up their lines. As they looked over the side, they could see them coming up through the clear water. They watched as the mackerel came nearer to the surface. They were spinning like strips of silver paper. "They're coming!" shouted Jago, as he pulled in the first mackerel out and onto the deck. Denzil wasn't far behind with his line. They held their lines tightly and shook the fish off onto the deck. Treeve turned to Pirran saying, "I wish father was here to see this. I've never seen the boys so happy."

Their first fish had been landed on the deck; there was no stopping them now. As soon as the lines were up and cleared of fish, they went back over and down into the sea. All four of them had been steadily catching fish; the decks of the Acorn were slowly filling up. By now the other half of the fleet had joined them; the sea was beginning to feel a very crowded and busy

44

place. Every now and again the boats were so close to each other they would have to be pushed apart, to stop them bumping together. Treeve and Pirran knew most of the fishermen, throughout the morning they had been congratulated many times on building such a fine looking boat. It was like a game of musical chairs out there, with the boats moving around swopping positions, each trying to stay on the fish.

They had been fishing for almost two hours and the boys were looking tired. Their initial enthusiasm had been slightly dampened by all the hard work. The deck of the Acorn was now nearly knee deep in fish. The deck pounds were about half full. Treeve quietly spoke to Pirran, "I think we should go in now, the boys look pretty tired." Pirran chuckled to himself, "I don't know about them, my arms are ready to drop off!" "Yes," agreed Treeve, "Mine are feeling the same. Come on boys I think we've got enough for today. Pull your lines in and we'll make our way back to Newlyn. Let's go and weigh in the catch." Denzil and Jago were relieved to hear that and wasted no time pulling in their lines. "I think we all deserve a nice cup of tea now." said Treeve as he went into the wheelhouse and brought out a big flask of tea, and a large box of sandwiches Karenza had made for them.

Slowly they edged the Acorn out of the fleet. Once clear they turned, opened up the throttle and headed toward Newlyn. By now Denzil and Jago were slumped against the back of the boat, sitting amongst the mackerel they'd landed. The fish were almost up to their waists, completely covering their legs! "Come on," Treeve shouted to the boys, "No time for sleeping, there's work to be done when we get back to Newlyn. We have to sort the fish into their different sizes." "What do you mean?" asked Denzil, "I

45

thought all we had to do was put the fish into boxes and put them onto the market." "No such luck," replied Treeve "all the fish have to be graded into their sizes, small, medium and large. Looking at the amount of fish we have here we've a lot of grading to do. We still won't be finished then, we have to get all the fish from the boat onto the quay wall and then onto one of the market lorries. The fish will need to be weighed, ice added and tickets with our name on, 'The Acorn', put on each of the boxes. Finally the boxes will have to be put in the chilling room." "Oh," said Jago sagging, "I don't think I'll be able to make it! " "Nor me!" added Denzil. Treeve and Pirran had a good laugh, "Never mind," said Treeve, "It will only take us about an hour to get them sorted, and then both of you can have a well deserved rest, go into the wheelhouse and drink your tea and eat some sandwiches."

When they had landed the fish and weighed each box, there was just one task left to do - to wash the boat down and put her back on her moorings. All week Denzil and Jago had been washing and cleaning the boat but now, when it had to be done, they were almost falling asleep. They assured their fathers they would be up first thing next day and give it a good clean. Treeve and Pirran were sympathetic and let them sit this one out while they gave the boat a quick wash down themselves. "How much did we catch?" Jago asked his father. "We did very well indeed, considering it was our first trip. We had over one hundred and twenty stones of fish, so you both have a bit of money to go into your savings account." answered Pirran. The two boys smiled at each other, they were feeling very pleased with themselves and their lovely new boat.

That night they all had a good sleep, including Treeve and Pirran. They hadn't let on to the boys but they were just as tired as them by the time they got home! Next morning when Denzil and Jago got up they were suffering all sorts of aches and pains and had some difficulty standing up straight. They had muscles aching they didn't know they had! Even though the boys were aching nothing could keep them away from their beloved Acorn.

Chapter 7

Four years have passed since the Acorn was launched; Denzil and Jago are now fourteen. It is the start of the school summer holidays and the boys are looking forward to spending as much time as possible on the Acorn. She still looks as good new and is still on her mooring in Newlyn harbour. Although only fourteen they have become very proficient in boat handling. They now take mackerel fishing in their stride and over the past four years have earned a fair amount of money. With the money they've saved they have bought some new fishing equipment. The first things they bought were five wicker baskets of long lines. Each basket has a line of rope with two hundred hooks attached to it. Each of the hooks are neatly arranged around the rim of the basket, each hook being stuck into the band of cork that was sewn around the edge of the basket. All the hooks are set in order, so when they're sent trailing out over the back of the boat they won't tangle or cross over one another.

The next new addition they wanted to buy was a line-hauler, which they would need to pull their lines back up from the seabed and onto the boat. After seeing one of these linehaulers advertised for sale locally they asked their fathers if they could take them to look at it. It was a good buy, so the boys used the remainder of their savings and bought it. It didn't take their fathers long to install it on the Acorn, the boys were well pleased with their purchase. With this new equipment there weren't many weekends they missed fishing. Treeve and Pirran were considering allowing the boys take

48

the boat out by themselves throughout the school summer holidays. They had an order to build another new boat, just like the Acorn, this would mean they wouldn't be able to spare so much time to go fishing with the boys. If they took on the new build most of their time would be taken up in the boatshed. A local fishermen had been so impressed with the Acorn he'd asked them to build him an identical boat. They knew they were able build him one that looked like the Acorn, but they also knew there could only be one Acorn.

Karenza and Tegan were not particularly happy about letting the boys go out alone, but Treeve and Pirran reassured them the boys were quite capable. They explained to them the boys were very safety conscious and they had complete trust in them and the boat. Then Pirran came up with an idea, as the Acorn had a ship to shore radio on board, what if they put a radio in the boatshed as well, then they could keep in touch with the boys at all times. Tegan and Karenza seemed a bit easier with this suggestion so they reluctantly agreed to let them do it. Pirran added as long as the boys were back in the harbour by an agreed time and they kept in touch on the radio, they would be safe to go out to sea by themselves.

While this conversation was going on Denzil and Jago had been in the other room listening from behind the door. They thought nobody knew they were there, they both had their ears pressed up against the door. It suddenly went very quiet in the room, the talking had stopped, they glanced at each other, looking puzzled. Suddenly there was a click and the door opened and the boys fell into the room! Their mums and dads stood laughing at them; they knew the boys had been listening behind the door all the time!

"Well, "said Treeve, "I've no doubt you two have heard everything we have been talking about. Are you happy now?" Their faces said it all, they were grinning from ear to ear! They ran over to their mums and gave them both a big hug and thanked them for their trust in them saying, "Don't worry we'll be careful." The boys continued to reassure them. Of course Treeve and Pirran, weren't that worried for their safety at all, because they knew as long as they were on the Acorn they would be safe hands, they were sure the Acorn would always look after them.

The next day at the crack of dawn the boys were back at the boat. They set their V.H.F. radio to channel six and waited for their fathers' first transmission to them. Treeve connected the last wire to the radio in the boatshed and it came to life. Pirran picked up the microphone, pressed the button and began saying, "Acorn, Acorn, Acorn, this is the boatshed, do you receive? Over," Denzil and Jago nearly jumped out of their skins when the call came through the speaker! They had the volume set on full to make sure they didn't miss their dad's first call to them. When his voice came out through the speaker it was so loud it even frightened the seagulls who showed their disapproval with a chorus of loud squawking! Denzil picked up the handset and nervously pressed the button, and he replied, "Yes, this is the Acorn, receiving you loud and clear, over." Even though the boys had listened to their fathers using boat radios many times before, this was the first time they had ever used it themselves. "Hello, is that you Denzil?" asked Pirran. "Yes, I hear you, you're coming through loud and clear, it's sounding very good, over. Just a minute, dad, Jago wants to speak to you." He passed
50

the microphone over to Jago, " Is it alright if we take the boat out tomorrow and set out the long lines, the weather forecast is good and the winds will be very light so the sea will be calm?" After a little pause, Pirran and Treeve agreed. "Yes, all right," answered Pirran, "but, remember what we agreed, you will have to keep in touch with us on the radio, if you have any problems you must let us know immediately." "Fantastic," shouted back the boys as they cheered with delight. "Well," said Jago "we had better sign off now and we will start to put the long lines onto the boat ready for tomorrow. We'll see you at home teatime. Over and out."

Next morning the boys were up before first light. They rowed over to the boat, started up the engine, cast off the mooring lines and soon they were on their way out through the harbour gaps. This was a big day for the boys, it was their first time out without their fathers being with them, but they knew they would be watching them from the hillside as the Acorn left the harbour entrance. Although they had longed for the day when they could take the boat out by themselves, they couldn't help feeling very alone without their fathers being there with them, they would have to be making all the decisions for themselves.

They began entering into Mounts Bay, heading toward the Low Lee buoy. Their plans were to head west following Cornwall's beautiful coastline towards Lands End. When they were nearing Tada Do lighthouse, they needed to stop so that they could catch some mackerel for the bait on the hooks. They were about a mile from the shore; they stopped the engine, put their mackerel feathers down over the side of the boat and began jigging. They were lucky, within a few minutes they had caught enough for the bait.

51

Denzil started the engine again and they continued heading along the coast, passing Lamorna cove, the Minack theatre, Penberth carrying on past the Longships lighthouse and on towards Wolf Rock lighthouse. Jago stayed on deck and prepared the bait ready for the hooks. They were heading for a piece of rough ground that had been recommended to them by another fisherman friend of their fathers. He had given them landmarks to take bearings from; these would make sure they were at the right spot to put their long lines out. They were about halfway between Lands End and the Wolf Rock. All they had to do now was line up the landmarks. They had to look for a specific large tree and then line it up with white farmhouse behind it. Denzil eyed the landscape like an old fisherman. When they had the marks near enough in line, he shouted to Jago to get the anchor and the marker buoy ready. The marker buoy was like a big orange football attached to a long length of rope, this was called an end line, it had an anchor attached to the end. When anchored out this buoy would give them a permanent position without them having to refer to any landmarks. Denzil called to Jago, who was ready and waiting on deck with the anchor and coil of end line. It was loosely coiled so that it would run out of the boat tangle free. "Ok, Jago, Let her go!" called Denzil. Jago threw the anchor over the stern of the boat into the sea, and the coil quickly followed it until the anchor reached the seabed. Jago waited until the rope was nearly out then he threw out the orange marker buoy. Denzil put the gear lever into the forward position, and the boat slowly moved ahead and the first of the long lines went trailing out over the stern of the boat.

The rest of the baskets were all baited up and ready to do the same thing. As the lines trailed out Jago had to carefully and slowly rotate the baskets ensuring the hooks left the basket in the right order with no tangles. Denzil, still in the wheelhouse, was keeping a close eye out for Jago as he turned the baskets, just in case something went wrong. Long line hooks can be very dangerous, if one catches into you on its' way out of the boat it could easily pull you out with it. By watching closely he would be able to stop the boat immediately if this should happen. Everything went well and they were near the end of the first basket of hooks. The last of the hooks was approaching, Jago stood ready with the end anchor, as the last of the hooks went out over stern he threw the anchor over into the sea. The coil of rope whizzed out after it, followed by the marker buoy. They worked well as a team and it didn't take them long to set the other four baskets off in exactly the same way. The weather had turned out fine; the bright blue sea had no more than a ripple on it. Now all they had to do was to sit and wait five hours and hope for the best.

Denzil said, "I think we should radio the boatshed and let them know everything is going well." Denzil picked up the microphone and said; "Boatshed, boatshed, boatshed, this is Acorn, do you receive? Over" "Yes we receive you ok, is everything going alright?" replied Pirran. "Yes, we've set all of our lines, everything went very well, we didn't have any hitches at all, we will be pulling them back up in about four hours time." "Very good," said Treeve, "let's hope you get some fish on them!" "We'll have to wait and see," said Denzil, "but we are feeling lucky!" "Alright we'll leave you to it now. Give us a call later and let us know how things are going." "Right, will do, over and out," said Denzil.

The boys decided as it was such a nice day they might as well do a bit of sunbathing now the deck was clear. They stripped off down to their underpants and stretched out on the deck. It was lovely and warm, they looked up into the sky. They lay with their hands behind their heads, the Acorn swayed gently as the little wavelets slapped against the side of the hull. They just laid there looking up into the cloud free blue sky enjoying the moment. Denzil said quietly, "You know, we are very lucky aren't we, there aren't many boys of our age who are lucky enough to own a boat like this." "I know," agreed Jago," Fantastic isn't it!" He raised himself up into to a sitting position, he scanned around looking at the boat and thought – yes, she is a nice looking boat isn't she, yes we are very lucky indeed. He lay back down on the deck and smiled with a look of contentment on his face. They lay there for about twenty minutes enjoying the sunshine when suddenly Jago sat up, as if startled by something he said, "Did you hear something then Denzil?" "No, I didn't hear anything" he replied with a concerned look on his face, "What sort of sound was it?" "Never mind," said Jago, "I must have imagined it." and he lay back onto the deck. No sooner had he had laid back down, then it happened again, except this time both of them heard it. First there was a bump it seemed to come from under the boat. It was followed by a scraping sound coming from the bottom of the boat. They jumped up and ran to either side of the boat to see if they could see anything, they were getting a little concerned. Neither had a clue what these sounds could be, then it happened again, except this time the bump was much louder, again it

54

was followed by a scraping sound. It was a bit scary. "I'm going to climb up onto the wheelhouse roof and see if I can see anything from up there." said Jago

He climbed up onto the wheelhouse roof, holding onto the small mast, whilst shielding his eyes from the sun's glare with his other hand. Looking all around the boat he couldn't see anything. The sun was very bright and the sea was calm making it difficult for him to see through the reflection of the sun on the water. He climbed back down onto the deck and they both stood in silence, listening. It had stopped, whatever it was making the noises, seemed to have gone away. Then, with no warning, the water along the port side of the boat erupted with a loud whooshing sound and out of the sea flew a large dolphin! He came up out of the water jumping clean over the boat. They both immediately dived down onto the deck, wasting no time getting out of the way. They were showered with a spray of salt water. As they lay on the deck they found themselves looking up at a huge dolphin passing above them. They were amazed, it had all happened so quickly. The dolphin landed back into the sea on the starboard side of the boat making a huge splash. The boys looked at each other, their hearts pounding but laughing their heads off at the same time! "What do you suppose that was all about?" said Denzil "I don't know." replied Jago, still laughing. They slowly raised their heads up to look over the side of the boat and they saw a big smiley face looking back up at them. They looked at one another and burst out laughing again. "It's a dolphin, he must been playing with the bottom of the boat! He must have been rubbing his body along the bottom of the boat and that was the scrapping sound we heard. Look at him Jago, he looks like he's laughing at us," said Denzil "Yes, he looks like he's smiling doesn't he." Jago added. "Yes, he does," agreed Denzil.

The dolphin gently rolled over showing his big white under belly. He was really close to them, right alongside the boat, the boys just stood there looking down at him, he was so beautiful. Denzil reached his hand out over the gunnels and began touching and stroking his belly, he seemed to like this. Jago joined in, they were both smoothing and stroking him. "He's very friendly, isn't he" said Denzil. "He's fantastic!" exclaimed Jago. The dolphin slowly rolled back into the water until only his head was showing above the surface. As the boys looked at him they could see their reflection in his beautiful eyes. Then, with a flick of his tail, he was gone, disappearing back down into the sea. The boys felt sure they hadn't seen the last of him, but several hours passed and there was still no sign of him, they assumed he must have lost interest in them and gone back about his daily business somewhere else in the sea.

They decided it was time to go back and pull up their lines. Denzil started the engine and they headed the boat back to their first marker buoy. They were about a mile away as the boat had been drifting along with the tide. As they approached the first marker buoy Jago stood waiting to grab it with the boat hook. Denzil edged in the Acorn closer toward the buoy, it was nearly within reach and Jago was ready to grab it, when it suddenly it disappeared down into the sea! "It's gone!" shouted Jago in amazement. Denzil knocked the boat out of gear and came out to take a look. "You're right Jago, it's gone!" Then, just as suddenly it popped up again, except this time it came flying out of the water and landed on the deck of the boat! They

56

both jumped out of the way in case it hit them! They weren't sure what had happened, then, guess who poked his head out of the water, it was the dolphin, he was back, with a big smile on his face and chirping away! But this time the boys didn't have the time to play with him. Now was the time they needed to catch some fish. Jago put the marker buoy line around the line hauler and began pulling up the end line. As the line came up the dolphin moved closer to see what was coming up. It didn't take long before the anchor was up. Jago placed it to one side at the stern of the boat and began hauling up the main line. Denzil was on the deck ready to start helping Jago take the fish from the line. The dolphin moved in even closer as if to watch the fish coming up on the line. Maybe he was waiting for something that took his fancy, like a free meal said Jago!

The boys were surrounded by squawking seagulls; they were circling the boat in anticipation of an easy feed that might fall from the line. As the first fish came out of the water the volume of the gulls increased, it was as if they were sending a message out to every bird in the area "dinner is being served!" The first fish to come up was a big codfish, about sixteen pounds in weight. Jago quickly grabbed the line and snatched the hook from it's mouth. The next one was a big fat conger eel. It must have been all of thirty pounds. Jago was not very keen on conger eels. You have to be careful with big congers, given a chance they would have a piece of you in their mouth and they're not particular which part of you they grab! Jago stopped the hauler and pulled the hook from its mouth. Denzil pulled the control lever on the hauler and they were back in action. The fish were coming up fast and furious, monkfish, ling, plaice, ray. There was a fish on almost every hook.

57

The deck pounds were filling fast and this was only the first line! Jago said jokingly, "If it continues like this we will have to ask another boat to come out and take some, we won't have enough room if it carries on like this!"

They were coming to the end of the line, towards the end marker buoy and then the anchor. All this time the dolphin was watching everything that was going on. Jago shouted to him, "Come on then Mr Dolphin, if you want to do something useful, throw in the marker buoy to us!" They both laughed, but, to their surprise, the dolphin went straight to the buoy and put it under his nose and flicked it up into the boat. "I can't believe my eyes." said Jago," he actually did what I asked him to do!" Jago shouted back to the dolphin, "Thanks a lot for that, don't go away, you can help with the rest!" The dolphin replied by chirping and doing another a lovely back flip. The boys could hardly believe what they were seeing; the dolphin actually seemed to understand what they were saying to him. Denzil put the rope over the line hauler and began to pull up the rest of the end line with the anchor. Jago started to the sort the fish into the deck pounds. The anchor was up and they were ready to start the next line. Both were well pleased with the amount of fish they had caught. The boys quickly put the line back into the basket, setting it to one side ready to use again. They were ready to haul up the next string. As they approached the next marker buoy the dolphin was already there waiting for them to arrive. "Do you think he will do it again?" said Denzil. "I don't know, I hope he does, it'll save us a lot of work! said Jago. He shouted to the dolphin. "Come on then, throw us in the marker buoy, we're ready." The dolphin went straight to the marker buoy and flicked it up into the boat. "This is fantastic, it looks like we have a new crewman!"
58

The boys went into action again, there were fish coming up on every hook. They worked their way through the line and as they approached the end marker buoy, the dolphin was there ready and waiting for them. "Right then," shouted Denzil, "throw it in to us." The dolphin put the buoy under his snout and with a quick flick it came hurdling towards the boat, this time Jago caught it in mid air! "How's that!" he shouted. "Good catch!" said Denzil. "This is getting to be good fun!" Even the dolphin seemed to be applauding at Denzil's catch. He came shooting out of the water and did a double summersault, crashing down alongside the boat, showering them with water!

Denzil pulled in the anchor while Jago sorted the fish. Along with their newly found friend, they made their way over to the next string as they grew nearer to it, up it came again, with perfect accuracy straight onto the deck. The dolphin gave his usual chirps, followed by a back flip. The same thing happened on the next two lines, every time the dolphin threw in the buoy onto the boat, and every time the line was full of fish. They had so much fish on board it was pushing the boat deep and deeper into the water with the weight. Denzil shouted over to the dolphin, it was time for them to go home and perhaps they might see him another day. "Yes," said Jago, "Yes, you can come out and help us anytime you want to." The dolphin raised himself out of the water balancing himself on his tail in a back and forth motion, while his beak like mouth chattered away merrily. "He is certainly good with the tricks, isn't he." said Jago. "He's a beauty!" said Denzil.

The boys squeezed their way in through the door of the wheelhouse, making sure none of the conger eels got in there with them! Denzil turned the key and started the engine; they were ready to head for home. It was a good thing the sea was calm, the Acorn could not have handled much more weight. As they looked out from the wheelhouse they could see the dolphin in front of them jumping in and out of the sea. It seemed he hadn't finished showing them his full repertoire of tricks. He was doing summersaults and spinning around in mid air. You name it he was doing it! As the Acorn drew nearer to Newlyn the dolphin swam in front of the boat. The boys decided they had better call the boatshed on the radio and let their fathers know they were on their way back. Jago picked up the microphone, "Boatshed, boatshed, boatshed, this is Acorn, do you receive, over?" "Yes Acorn, this is the boatshed. How have you done, did you catch much fish?" replied Pirran "You won't believe it till you see it!" replied Jago. "I think we'll need some help when we get back to the harbour. We have got so much fish on board it looks like the boat is sinking with the weight. Can you come down and help us when we get back in the harbour?" "Yes, what time do you think you'll get back in?" asked Pirran. "Well," said Jago," we are just coming up to Mousehole Island now, so I think we'll be there in about half an hour." "Right ok," said Pirran "we'll be on the fish market waiting for you when you get in." "Ok, see you soon." replied Jago, "Over and out."

The dolphin was still in front of the boat, as if he were leading the way home. As they neared the harbour he swam around to the side of the boat, looked up into the wheelhouse, gave two gentle chirps and dived down into the sea. The boys looked around for a while to see if he would reappear, but he had gone. "I wonder if we'll ever see him again." said Denzil. "I have a funny feeling we will." answered Jago. "I hope you're right." As they came
60

in through the harbour entrance they could see their fathers waiting on the quay for them, there was also a lot of other people there. The boys wondered what was happening. As they pulled up to the quay wall they noticed a man stood looking down at them, taking photos of them. They threw the ropes up to their fathers for them to tie off the boat. Jago asked his father "Who is the man on the quay taking the photos of us." "He's from the Daily Recorder; he's come to talk to you both. He wants to tell the story about your big catch." said Pirran "Never mind the fish, wait till we tell him about the dolphin that's been helping us all day." said Jago. "A dolphin." said Pirran "How has a dolphin been helping you?" "Well, for a start he picked up and threw us every marker buoy out of the water and onto the boat. It wouldn't surprise us if he had something to do with the amount of fish we've caught as well" said Jago. "I think I'm inclined to agree with you, it's a long time since anybody has caught so much fish with just five baskets of lines," said Treeve. "That's why so many people are here. Someone heard us speaking on the radio and one thing leads to another, you know what it's like." replied Pirran.

It was a good feeling landing all the fish. All four of them worked hard for about two hours, and landed over four hundred stone of mainly prime fish. That surely had to be a port record for two fourteen-year-old boys! The reporter spoke to the boys and took down all the details of their trip including the part the dolphin played, thanking them he said, "This is going to make a very interesting story, so make sure you both read the paper tomorrow, this will be going straight to press." The last of the fish was put into the chillers, all ticketed and iced up ready to be sold the next morning. Pirran put his arm around Jago's shoulder saying "Well, it looks like you are both going to be famous!" They all had a good laugh and began to make their way home.

They had decided to leave the Acorn tied against the quay wall for the night and put her on her moorings in the morning. When they arrived home the boys were full of themselves, their spirits were high, over and over again they told the story of the dolphin. Although their mums hadn't been too keen on letting them go fishing alone, they felt very proud of their sons. Treeve said to Pirran, "What do you think about this dolphin? Have you ever heard of dolphins doing anything like this before? It must be a very clever fish."

Chapter 8

Next morning the boys were up early and were making their way down to the boat. They could see the fish market and it seemed very busy. All their boxes of fish were neatly out on the floor of the market. The boys' fish was about to be auctioned. This was a very exciting time for the boys, and a proud moment for their parents. The fish market was mainly operated by one local family. This family also had a large fleet of beam trawlers. It just so happen most of these trawlers were also landing their fish, so the market had a lot of fish to be auctioned that day. The bell sounded to signal the start of the auction. It was a very exciting time for Denzil and Jago. The hustle and bustle, the sounds of the auctioneers and buyers shouting out their bids. The auctioneers' words were almost unrecognizable as they were speaking so quickly. Most people on the outside of the fishing industry would not have been able to understand them at all, but it was a great atmosphere!

As the boys watched the auction they overheard two men in front of them talking, one said to the other, "Is it right that two fourteen year olds caught most of this fish?" "Yes, that's right," affirmed his companion, "not a bad catch is it, what's the name of the boat they were on?" "I don't know" was the reply. On hearing this Denzil just couldn't help himself, he had to tell them. "It was the Acorn." he said The two men turned around and looked toward them. The boys were feeling very small amongst all these grownups. One of the men said, "I bet you wish you could catch that amount of fish don't you?" The boys looked at each other and started to giggle. "What's the matter with you two" said the man "did I say something funny?" "Oh no" replied Jago, "we just thought of something funny that's all" The two men turned their back on the boys. Then the one said to the other, "Kids, you never know what's going on in their minds do you." "Come on then," said Jago to Denzil, "let's go and put the Acorn back on her moorings." When the two men heard this they immediately turned around to see who had spoken. " Did you hear that," one said to the other, "they must be the boys who caught all that fish!"

The boys climbed down the ladder on the side of the quay wall and aboard the Acorn. Denzil untied the mooring ropes while Jago unlocked wheelhouse and started up the engine. Denzil pushed her off from the wall and she gently chugged toward her mooring. As they were leaving they could see the two fish merchants they'd spoken to earlier watching them. The boys gave them a smile and a wave, the men hesitated for a moment but then smiled back and gave them a wave. The boys tied the Acorn on her mooring and spent the rest of day tidying, cleaning and disinfecting her decks. The long lines had been sorted and checked, making sure each hook was put in exactly the right place around the rim of the basket. They planned to go out again within a few days if the weather was good. They both hoped to see the dolphin again and they were anxious to go back out to sea and do it all over again.

When they arrived home that evening they had a pleasant surprise. Their parents were waiting for them with the evening paper. "You're on the front page! "said Treeve, holding up the newspaper " Look you made the headlines." It read, 'Boys make record catch at Newlyn'. "It went on to tell

64

when and where they had caught the fish with the help of a dolphin. The boys felt ten feet tall. Seeing their names in the local paper, made them feel like celebrities! As they read on their spirits came crashing down to earth. The article went on to say that 'two marine experts were very interested in the dolphin saying they had plans to capture him and take him to their Zoo in the Midlands. They were particularly interested in the acrobatics he could do, and they hoped to be in Cornwall within the next few days. They said they would be building a special tank where he would be put on display entertaining lots of people. "They can't do that!" shrieked Jago. "No they can't" agreed his father, "anyway I think the dolphin will be too smart for them." "It's all our fault," said Denzil, "we shouldn't have said anything about the dolphin. Now he'll have all sorts of people chasing him around, trying to catch him, just to lock him away in a small pond. All because we opened our big mouths, he could lose his freedom!" Treeve reassured them, "Don't worry, they probably won't come down. Don't worry about it, you know what newspapers are like, they print anything that makes a good story," "Anyway, the dolphin might be gone by now." added Treeve. But he and Pirran were secretly thinking, this dolphin was much more important than the boys could possibly know. They took comfort in remembering what had happened to them and their father all those years before. They knew no harm would come to the boys or the dolphin, the Acorn would see to that.

As the boys left the harbour the next day they were hoping to see the dolphin again, but at the same time hoping he had gone away so he would be safe and never caught. But they were getting excited at the thought they might see him again. They were about a hundred yards out from the harbour entrance when the dolphin popped out of the sea. "There he is!" shouted Jago," look he's right at the side of the boat.' Denzil eased back on the throttle and they went to say hello to him. He popped his head out of the water and gave a long excited chatter as if he were telling them he was glad to see them as well. As he came in close the boys reached over and smoothed him. He rolled over belly side up, this was where he liked to be stroked the most! "I wonder why he comes to our boat?" pondered Denzil, "After all there must be hundreds of boats working in this area, yet nobody else has ever seen him." The dolphin raised his head and looked up at them as if he understood every word they were saying. He opened his mouth and gave them a multi-toned chatter. "I'm sure he's talking to us," said Jago. "Yes," agreed Denzil , "I think he is talking to us, it's a shame we don't know how to speak dolphin!" he shouted toward the dolphin saying, "you must go away! There are some men coming down here, they are going to try and catch you and put you into a Zoo." The dolphin dived down into the water with a quick flick of his tail, as if he understood everything. He came back up to the surface, raised his head out of the water and shook it from side to side as if he was saying "No" " Incredible!" said Jago, " really incredible, he does understand every word we say to him!" Denzil spoke to him again, "will you go away." He looked up at the boys and shook his head again as if saying "No". The boys looked at each other in amazement. "Does that mean you'll be staying then?" asked Denzil. Again the dolphin shook his head, except this time it was up and down as if he were saying "Yes". The boys could hardly believe it, they were actually talking to a dolphin! "Don't worry we won't let them catch you." They reassured him. The dolphin replied with

66

another chatter. "We should give him a name," said Jago," we can't keep calling him dolphin." "Yes we should," agreed Denzil.

"As he always looks like he's smiling, why don't we call him Smiley." "Yes" said Jago, "that's a great name." They turned toward the dolphin who was looking up at them, he looked like he was listening to every word they were speaking. "Do you like the name Smiley?" asked Jago, "would you be happy with that name?" The dolphin nodded his head up and down as if he was in agreement with them, chirping and chattering away. "Well, it looks like he's happy with his new name. Right then Mr Dolphin from now on your name will be Smiley." Smiley shook his head up and down in approval. Denzil shouted to him, "Ok, Smiley, it is time for us to do some fishing, are you coming with us?" Smiley nodded his head up and down, and dived down into the sea. The boys had never felt happier than they did at that moment. "Just think," said Denzil, "we must be the only boys in the world with a talking dolphin for a friend!" "Well not quite a talking dolphin, Jago, but he's pretty good at nodding his head!"

This time the boys decided they would try their luck on the eastern side of the bay about a mile off the Lizard Point. Off they went with the Acorn gently pushing its way through the sea, pitching up and down making its' way through the waves, rolling gently from side to side. Smiley took up his usual position at the front of the boat, gracefully diving up and down through the clear blue sea. He seemed to be making very little effort, the waves just slid over him as if he wasn't there. As they were watching Smiley Jago said to Denzil, "How could anybody consider locking him away in a Zoo? I just can't understand why anybody would want to put such a beautiful creature into captivity, just to make money, it doesn't seem right. Out here he has freedom and the whole sea as his playground." "Don't worry," replied Jago, "I think Smiley is much too clever to let anybody catch him." "Yes, I think you're right, he is definitely a clever dolphin!" said Denzil.

As they made their way out, every now and then Smiley would dive in and out of the water in front of them, leaping up into the air, doing big belly flops. It looked like he was really enjoying himself. He also went to the stern playing in the wake, always being careful not to get too close to the propeller. They decided to set out their lines about a mile south off Lizard Point. This area was known as a good fishing ground. Denzil put the gear lever into neutral and the throttle into tick over. He went out on deck to help Jago get the lines ready for shooting. Smiley seemed to have disappeared for a moment, but no doubt he would be back again. Jago picked up the anchor ready to throw it into the sea. Just as he was about to throw it in, Smiley popped up alongside the boat. He looked up at Jago and shook his head back and forth. "It looks like he's saying no Denzil. I think he's telling us not to put the lines out here." "Is that what you're saying to us Smiley?" asked Denzil ''Well Smiley where shall we put them?" asked Jago. Smiley flicked his tail and started to swim off in front of the boat. "I think he wants us to follow him." "So let's do it then." urged Denzil. Jago put the Acorn back into gear and headed after Smiley. They followed him, they were heading further out to sea, after a few miles Smiley disappeared down into the sea. The boys waited with the Acorn in neutral gear, waiting for Smiley to appear.

They didn't have to wait long before Smiley was back, he swam alongside the boat. He gave the boys an excited chattering sound and shook

68

his head up and down. "Shall we put our lines out here? "asked Jago. Smiley shook his head up and down as if saying "Yes". Jago and Denzil were finding it hard to believe what was happening, not only did they have a dolphin that spoke to them, but he was also taking them to where the fish were as well! Jago threw over the first anchor. The baited hooks went trailing out over the stern of the boat and were on their way down to the seabed. Within an hour all the lines were out. Now all they had to do was wait a while before they could haul them back in. As they waited they watched Smiley playing with the marker buoys. He was gently poking and prodding them with his beak-like nose, trying to flick them into the air. The boys decided to get one of their old buoys from the wheelhouse and see if he wanted to play ball with them. Jago picked up the buoy and threw out towards Smiley. Immediately upon hearing it hit the water he was on his way to it. Denzil shouted to Smiley to throw it back. The buoy must have been about twenty yards away from the boat. Smiley came up right underneath it and with a flick of his head the buoy came careering out of the water straight into Jago's hands. "What a shot!" shouted Denzil clapping his hands with delight. Smiley was half out of the water balancing on his tail, wriggling it back and forth very fast as if he was excited and he was asking for more! Jago threw the buoy back out and to their amazement it hardly touched the water. As soon as Smiley saw it coming he positioned himself right underneath it and caught it on the end of his nose! "I think he's trying to show us that we are not the only ones who can catch a ball" laughed Jago. With another flick from his head the ball was again on its way back to the Acorn.

This fun and games went on for about an hour and they all had great fun. Suddenly Smiley dived down into sea. "He must be fed up with the game of catch and has gone for a swim somewhere" said Jago. It was then they realised why Smiley had dived down into the water. Coming straight towards them was the biggest sharks' fin they had ever seen. All the splashing in the water when they had been playing with Smiley must have attracted the shark toward them. It probably wanted to see what the disturbance in the water was about. "It looks like the fin of an extremely large Porbeagle shark," said Jago. Denzil, agreed. Although Porbeagle sharks were pretty common around the coast of Cornwall they had never seen or heard of one being as big as this one, it was really big! They watched it as it circled the boat. It didn't look at all friendly; it was much bigger than Smiley, perhaps this was why he had gotten out of way! Sharks didn't usually bother dolphins, mainly because dolphins tended to keep out of their way just in case!

The shark didn't stay around for very long, he must have sized up the Acorn and decided it was too big to eat so he made off into the distance. As soon as the shark was a safe distance away Smiley reappeared alongside. Jago shouted to him, "What's the matter with you, don't you like sharks?" Smiley quickly replied, nodding his head from side to side, meaning a definite "No!" They both had a good laugh. "I think it's time we hauled in the lines." said Denzil. Jago agreed, he went into the wheelhouse and started up the engine and they made their way over to the first marker buoy. Smiley was already waiting there to throw up the buoy onto the boat. As the boat came alongside, up it came and the boys and Smiley went into their usual routine. "It looks like good fishing again," said Jago. "I don't think we can fail to catch fish with Smiley taking us to where they are." said Denzil.

All four lines were now aboard the boat and the fishing was as good as their first trip. They approached the last marker buoy, and they were expecting Smiley to be there waiting for them. They waited a few minutes but nothing happened, he wasn't there. "Never mind," said Denzil "he will probably be back soon," Jago picked up the long boat hook he reached out and grabbed the last line and marker buoy. Denzil put the line into the hauler and started to winch it up. All was going well, with only half the line on board the pounds were already almost full. When suddenly there was an almighty splashing and crashing alongside the boat. It was the shark, he was back! He had decided he was going to help himself to the fish on the line. He pulled and jerked on the line with such force he pulled the line out from the hauler. This shark wasn't happy with just taking one fish he wanted them all! He had worked himself up into a feeding frenzy and he had managed to tangle himself up in the line and the hooks. This made a bad situation even worse every time he struggled to try and free himself it got worse. Jago had lost control of the line, as it flew out of the hauler it began to fly back out of the boat at high speed. He tried to get out of the way of the empty hooks but as the line was being pulled out so quickly a few of the hooks caught in his jumper. Before he could do anything about it he was being pulled out over the side of the boat into the sea. Suddenly the line came to a halt. It had become tight, the line had managed to tangle itself around the hauler bringing the line to a sudden stop. Denzil looked on helplessly as he watched Jago struggling in the water trying to get the hooks from his jumper. Denzil wasn't sure what to do next. "Throw me a lifebelt" shouted Jago, "if the shark dives down he will take me with him!" Denzil quickly threw the lifebelt towards Jago. Jago was about thirty yards away from the boat, the lifebelt landed just within his reach. As he reached out and took hold of it his fears had been right, the shark dived downwards, thrashing wildly, diving deeper into the water! Denzil watched helplessly as Jago disappeared down under the water. Denzil's stomach cramped with panic. He couldn't bear the thought of anything happening to Jago, yet there was nothing he could do! He held his breath in empathy with Jago, he pleaded with God to help him save Jago. His prayers were answered. Jago broke the surface coughing and gasping for air! The shark surfaced about twenty yards from him, still thrashing, getting himself into a frenzy. Denzil knew he had to get the hooks out of Jago's jumper. Jago pulled and tugged at the hooks for all he was worth, but they were well and truly tangled up. He needed a knife to cut himself free.

The shark started to swim away from the boat in a desperate attempt to free himself of the line. As it swam away the line snapped tight and the Acorn lurched. Denzil looked on in horror, there was still nothing he could do. Jago was holding onto the lifebelt for all he was worth, but Denzil could see he was getting tired. He shouted over to him, "Try to take your jumper off." "I can't, if I let go of the lifebelt I will lose it. I need a knife to cut myself free." Denzil knew, somehow he had to get a knife over to him, and he knew there was only one way to do that and that was to swim to him! He picked up a knife from the wheelhouse, as quickly as he could he slipped out of his oilskins to make it easier to swim. He dived straight over the side of the boat and started swimming towards Jago with the knife between his teeth.

He needed to cut the line on the other side of Jago, this would set the shark free and stop him pulling Jago back down under the water. He swam across to Jago as quickly as he could, he took the knife and managed to cut the line, Jago was free! They turned and swam back towards the boat .When they were both alongside the Acorn, they stretched up and held onto the gunnels, now all they needed to do was somehow get back on board the boat! Denzel said to Jago "you hang on there and I will climb up on to the boat." As he spoke Denzil noticed the sharks' fin re-appear and it was not far away! It must have freed itself from the line when Denzil cut it and was heading towards them. It was closing in on them fast, it was inches away from them! Suddenly there was a terrific thudding sound. It was the sound of the shark being lifted into the air, bent double as if he had been hit by a sledge hammer! Denzil shouted in triumph "It's Smiley!" He had rammed the shark from underneath with his nose at high speed! They could see the massive Porbeagle shark slowly sinking down into the sea, they looked at each other. "That was a close one, I wouldn't want to go through that again!" "You can say that again!" agreed Denzil. "Come on let's get ourselves back onto the boat where it's safe." Just then Smiley appeared alongside them and gave them a victory chatter. Jago gently patted him on the head "Smiley you're beautiful, another couple of inches and I'm sure the shark would have had one of us. We're really grateful to you." Smiley rolled over and showed his white belly, as if he was saying 'that's alright, anytime, it was nothing.' Jago couldn't help but laugh and he gave Smiley a good rub on his belly.

They clambered back on board the Acorn. Despite landing in amongst all the fish they were glad to be back aboard again. Denzil went into

73

the wheelhouse and fetched out the spare clothes they kept on board, just in case they ever got wet. Even though it was a warm sunny day the water was cold and they were glad to get into some dry clothes. "Time to go home." said Jago. "Yep, that sounds like a good idea." agreed Denzil. "I will radio in and let them know we are on our way back in." As they rounded the harbour entrance they could see their fathers stood on the quayside waiting for them. It doesn't take long for a crowd to gather at Newlyn. The boys' fathers looked down in disbelief when they saw how much fish they had on the boat. "How on earth did you catch that much? "shouted down Treeve. "What do you mean?" replied Denzil, "that's nothing. You should have seen the one that got away!" Both boys laughed and Treeve realised they were just teasing him. The boys threw up the mooring ropes to their dads, who tied them off on the quay.

Denzil and Jago climbed up the ladder onto the quay and began to tell their fathers what had happened to them. Pirran noticed the crowd had moved in closer and were listening to the boys. Jago had started to tell about the part the Smiley had played, his father knew he had to stop him, more publicity wouldn't help the Smiley at all. "Hang on boys, before you say any more I've got something over here I want you to see." He took the boys to one side and explained to it would best for them not to say anything more about Smiley. They realised he was right, further publicity would make the people from the Zoo even more interested. "We'll just get the fish landed and in the cooler, you can tell us all about it when we get back home" said Treeve. During the next hour, while they were landing their fish, everyone was keen to know how and where they had caught so many fish. Heeding

74

their fathers words, the boys simply answered; "They were on the line when we hauled in." But there were some in the crowd that had heard the boys start to tell their tale when they had first arrived. The boy's sudden change into a casual attitude made some of them even more inquisitive about how they had caught so much fish. Treeve and Pirran were not about to give them any more answers, so they were left to ponder.

At last all the fish were boxed and iced and put in the cooler on the fish market. The boys left the Acorn tied against the quay wall for the night and they all made their way home. The boys were busting to tell their dads' all about the days' events. After listening to the boy's account of the day Treeve and Pirran decided it would be best for the boys not to tell their mums about their ordeal with the shark. If they knew about that they would definitely not allow them to go out on their own again! When the boys had finished telling their story Treeve and Pirran were even more convinced the boys would always be in safe hands when they were out on the Acorn!

Chapter 9

When the boys arrived at the Acorn the next morning, there were two men waiting for them. The two men approached them. "Hello" said one of them, it's nice to meet you both, we have heard a lot about you two. You must be Jago and I presume you are Denzil." he said. "Yes, that's right." replied Jago. The boys glanced at each other wondering who these two men were. He then introduced himself "My name is Jack Evans and this is my partner Billy Johns. We wondered if we could have a chat with you about the dolphin that has been following you around." "What do you want to know about him?" asked Jago with a concerned look on his face. "Well, "said, Jack Evans." We have come down from the Midlands, where we own a small Zoo. We were looking into the possibility of capturing the dolphin and taking him back to our Zoo." Their worst fears were coming true. "What do you want to know about him?" enquired Denzil "not that we can tell you very much, we only saw him on that day and we haven't seen him since." Willy Johns quickly interrupted, "That's not true is it, we heard you say last night the dolphin was with you all day again. We were listening to you on this very spot, when you came in yesterday." The boys looked at each other, then Denzil said, "I think you must be mistaken we didn't say anything about the dolphin yesterday." "Look," said Willy Johns, "we don't want to hurt the dolphin, we just want to have a look at him. We wondered if you would be prepared to take us out on your boat for us to see him for ourselves?" "But that's the problem," said Jago, "you don't just want to look at him, do you? You want to capture him
76

and lock him away in some sort of tank. You want to take him to a Zoo for entertainment just so you can make more money." "What's wrong with that?" said, Jack Evans. "Well, we've got nothing against Zoos but we are pretty sure the dolphin would much prefer to stay in the open sea where he has his freedom to go wherever he chooses." said Denzil. "Look sonny, "said Willy Johns, with a more aggressive tone to his voice, "We are businessmen and a Zoo doesn't run on fresh air. If this dolphin is as clever as you have made him out to be, we want him. If you co-operate with us you will find that we are very generous people, we can pay you a lot of money to help us." "But you don't understand, we don't want your money" said Jago. "We would prefer it if you just left the dolphin alone." "Come on now, there's no sense you two taking that attitude. Just take a look around you, you're not the only ones in here who have a boat, everyone in the harbour is trying to earn money, everyone has their price. It's not going to take long for us to find somebody else to take us out and help us catch this fish. Come on, you need to see sense, we would rather work with you two. After all you are the ones who found the dolphin." said Jack Evans. "Sorry, we won't help you catch him, ever, so you had better go and find someone else to do your dirty work because we won't!" "Ok, if that's the way you want it's going to be your loss," snapped Willy Johns, "we've never had one we couldn't catch before! We will catch him somehow!" Denzil and Jago smiled at each other and replied together, "You haven't tried to catch this one before, have you?" With a scowling face Willy Johns snapped back "We'll have him before the week is out!" "We'll see," shouted back Denzil as they climbed down the ladder aboard the Acorn. They went into the wheelhouse both were wondering what to do next. One thing they did know, they couldn't let those people catch Smiley. For the moment they decided they would take a ride out into the bay and see if Smiley was out there waiting for them. As the Acorn passed through the harbour entrance Jago went up onto the foredeck and sat on the edge of the cabin roof to see if he could spot him anywhere. They headed out past Mousehole Island continuing further westward along the coast towards Lands End. They were about three miles out of Newlyn and still no sign of Smiley.

They were beginning to wonder if he had taken their advice and gone away. Then, as usual, out of the blue sea, up he came right alongside the boat with a big belly flop, sending a shower of water all over the boat, he seemed to like doing that to them! Denzil immediately pulled back on the throttle and put the Acorn into neutral. Jago rushed back down from the foredeck and both boys leaned over the side to see Smiley's grinning face poking out of the sea looking up at them. He was chattering away as if he was very excited to see them. They stretched over and smoothed and patted him, telling him how pleased they were to see him again. Smiley rolled over to show his white belly, he just loved his belly scratched and smoothed! For those few moments all three of them were happy and all thoughts of the horrible men from the Zoo were forgotten.

Suddenly Smiley became very uneasy, he rolled over into his normal swimming position and slowly submerged beneath the water. The boys waited, staring into the water expecting him to come back up at any moment. Just then Jago heard the sound of an engine in the distance. They both looked around. Sure enough there was a boat heading straight toward

78

them. It was about a hundred yards away, they could see, stood on the foredeck, somebody looking at them through binoculars. As the boat grew a little closer they recognised him. It was a local boat, one that worked from Newlyn gill netting, the skippers' name was Keith Moore. The man on the fore deck was joined by a second man, their faces became clear, it was the men from the Zoo, Billy Johns and Jack Evans! The boys' first thoughts were to warn Smiley, but he must have already known and was well out of the way. Denzil turned to Jago saying, "It didn't take them long to find another boat did it?" By now the other boat was coming up alongside. She was called Morning Star. Willy Johns and Jack Evans stood on the deck looking over towards the boys. Willy Johns with his big fat, shiny face that looked like a boiled egg, and his partner looking like a thin lipped ferret who had been sucking lemons! Willy Johns was smiling as he shouted over to them, "I told you it wouldn't take us long to find a boat, didn't I?" Jago replied. "Having a boat is one thing, catching this dolphin is another!" "Don't you worry," snapped back Willy Johns, "we'll get him, don't you worry about that. We know he's around here somewhere, it's only a matter of time before we get him. We know he was here with you, we could see him through our binoculars, and he was right alongside your boat." Just then Smiley came up in between the two boats. "Go away!" shouted Jago," they're trying to catch you!" But Smiley just stayed where he was giving a long chatter towards the two men on the Morning Star, then he dipped his head down into the water and sucked up a mouthful and sprayed both of them! He began shaking his head back and forth, as if he was telling them they had 'no chance'. The boys burst out laughing and shouted back over to them. "Do you still think you can catch him?" "Yes, we'll catch him," shouted back an angry, wet Willy Johns. "We'll prove to you that your dolphin's not as smart as you think he is. He's just lucky we haven't got any nets on board or we'd have him right now."

The two men were staring at Smiley, he stared right back at them. He swam up really closely, alongside them, almost close enough for them to touch him. The boys could see the excited look in the zookeepers eyes, now they wanted to catch him more than ever. Smiley flicked his tail and he showered them both again completely soaking them! They were not very amused at this and shouted, pointing down at him, "Soon you will be ours, you just wait and see. By the end of this week you'll be in our tank at the Zoo, then we'll see how you feel about making fools out of us." scowled fat Willy. Smiley gave them another long chatter as if challenging them, Denzil and Jago were almost crying with laughter. To make things even worse, the skipper of the Morning Star, had been watching from his cabin window, he was also doubled up with laughter. This infuriated the two men even more, they were shouting at Keith, instructing him to take them back to Newlyn and for him to stop laughing at them. "It's not funny, we're soaking!" protested Jack the ferret. The Morning Star turned and headed back towards Newlyn, but Smiley had not finished with them yet! He seemed to know he was getting to the two of them, so to rub salt in their wounds, he swam right alongside the Morning Star.

In the distance Denzil and Jago could see the two men shaking their fists at Smiley. They must have been shouting very loud at Smiley because the odd word could be heard travelling on the wind! The Morning Star was about two hundred yards away from the Acorn. As Denzil's father knew Keith very well, he decided he would give Keith a call on the radio. "Yes, this is Morning Star "replied Keith. But before Denzil could speak, Keith started to explain to him why he had taken the men from the Zoo on board his boat. He told them they had offered to pay him one hundred pounds a day and he needed the money. He hoped the two of them would understand. "Yes, "Denzil replied "it's ok, we understand. If you hadn't done it someone else would have." Keith was very pleased the boys didn't have any bad feelings towards him. He went on to assure the boys he wouldn't be doing any more than he had to do, he would just be taking orders from them. In other words he wouldn't be contributing any ideas on how to catch Smiley. "Look," said Keith, "I had better sign off now. I think they're about to come into the cabin and they wouldn't want to hear me talking to you about them, especially at the moment when they are still soaking wet! So I'll sign off for now and I'll see you later in the harbour." "Right oh," said Denzil, "we'll talk later, over and out."

The boys decided that for the moment they would stop fishing, because this would put Smiley in too much danger of being caught. It wouldn't take these men long to figure out how Smiley could easily be netted. Denzil and Jago weren't sure how the Zoo men intended to net Smiley, but thought it would more than likely they will be using mono nets. These nets are made of very thin nylon twine. This type of net is almost invisible when it's in the water, very similar to a Spider's web. Smiley would find it very difficult to see it and if he swam into it, he would find it impossible to get free. These nets are designed so the harder the fish try to escape the more entangled they become. So for the moment the boys would have to wait and see. They couldn't make any plans until they knew how Willy and Jack were going to try and catch Smiley. They decided to go back to Newlyn and watch to see what type of nets were being put aboard Morning Star, once they knew this they would know what to do.

It wasn't very long before Smiley was back alongside the Acorn chattering away. Jago called to Smiley and told him that he needed to be careful as these men were determined to catch him and take him to their Zoo. Smiley just chattered away as if he wasn't worried at all. The boys told him they had to go back into Newlyn and find out what type of nets the Zoo men were intending to use. They told him they'd be back the next day to see him. Smiley nodded in agreement and the boys headed back to Newlyn. As they entered the harbour they could see the Morning Star against the quay wall. The boys had been right, gill nets were being lowered onto her deck, this could present quite a problem for Smiley.

Chapter 10

Even though the boys were making an early start the next day, when they arrived the Morning Star had already left the harbour. They knew they had to get a move on to get out and find them, the battle of wits was about to begin. Wasting no time they released the mooring ropes and the Acorn was underway. "I feel very nervous about what they might be up to," said Denzil, "Yes," agreed Jago, "I hope Smiley is paying attention, he will need to be on full alert today."

The Acorn was about one mile off Newlyn, when Jago spotted a boat on the horizon. He took out his binoculars to see if he could make out who it was. Yes, it was the Morning Star. "Alright" said Denzil, "it seems to be stationary." The boys decided to have a closer look. As they grew nearer they could see two figures on top of the Morning Star's wheelhouse roof. It was the Zoo men, they were scanning the seas' surface, no doubt searching for Smiley. "Well that's a good sign" said Denzil. "If they're still looking it means they haven't found Smiley yet." The two zoo men had spotted the Acorn and they had their binoculars focused on them. Denzil was still looking at them through his binoculars, he gave them a wave, knowing it would irritate them! "Willy Johns is pointing his finger toward the Acorn," Jago turned to look, as he turned he saw Smiley alongside the Acorn. Denzil went over to greet him "Don't worry Smiley, we've thought up a few plans to stop them catching you. By the time we've finished with them they will be glad to get back home to the Midlands!"

Smiley didn't look at all bothered by the situation, if anything he was probably looking forward to having some fun with them. The two boats were getting closer, Jago noticed they had started shooting their nets over the stern of Morning Star. The boys were quite excited about having the chance to outwit these two mean characters. The first part of the boys' plan was to sit tight and let the Zoo men think they have a chance of encircling them with their nets. As the wind was coming from the West the conditions were perfect for what the boys were planning. Smiley could now be clearly seen from the Morning Star. As the boys predicted, the net was being set trying to encircle him. Denzil pulled the throttle back to slow the Acorn down; they didn't want to deter the men from continuing to set their net. Smiley stayed close to the side of the Acorn watching the activity. Denzil said to Jago, "I think it's time to get the rope ready, you explain to Smiley what part he has to play in our plan."

He went and pulled out a length of rope from the forward cabin locker. It was about thirty yards long and on each end of it he tied a small float. Jago went to the side of the boat to give Smiley his instructions. "Now this is what we want you to do Smiley," he began, "we need you to take one end of this rope in your mouth and pull it directly across the path of the Morning Star. When the rope is right in front of their bow, you let it go; the rope will do the rest! Do you understand?" Smiley nodded his head saying "Yes" "Right then, said Jago, "off you go" Jago placed one end of the rope in Smiley's mouth leaving the remainder trailing in the water. Smiley made his way over toward the Morning Star. The timing was perfect, the Morning Star was making its' final turn to complete the circle of net. Denzil and Jago

84

watched as Smiley got closer to her. He was about fifty yards away, none of the people on board had seen him, they were all too busy watching the Acorn and shooting their net. Smiley was now about twenty yards from her bow and right on course. The boys were pulling their hair out waiting for him to release the rope. Smiley was right on target, he let go of the rope directly in front of the Morning Star, turned and made his way back to the Acorn.

They could see the floats bobbing either side of her bow, nobody aboard had noticed a thing. As she passed over the rope, the two floats at either end would be pulled together and the rope dragged along their keel until it reached her propeller. Just as the boys expected it to do, the Morning Star came to a sudden halt! The boys jumped up and down cheering and began congratulating themselves – they'd won the first round! There was a great deal of panic on board Morning Star, everyone was hanging over the stern trying to see what had fowled the propeller. But the worst was yet to come, she was now at the mercy of the tide and wind. Behind her were hundreds of yards of netting which they were now unable to pull back in.

Slowly but surely the tide and the wind were bringing them and the net together, they had about ten minutes to free the propeller before the net would become completely entangled around them. If that were to happen there was no knowing how long it would take to get her free! As the Acorn moved in closer to the Morning Star they could see one of the men was starting to undress. It was Willy Johns, it looked like he was going to go over the side and try to pull the rope free from the propeller. The boys watched as he strapped on his diving gear, sat on the gunnels and slowly allowed himself to fall backwards into the water. They knew it wouldn't take him long to free the propeller with his diving gear on. Their plan had been to put the net out of action but if Willy Johns freed the propeller it wouldn't take them long before they got the net back in action and the whole operation to catch Smiley would start again.

Unknown to the boys, when he heard the splash of the diver hitting the water Smiley had gone over to the Morning Star. He swam underneath her to see what was going on. Willy Johns was at the propeller trying to untangle the rope from it, Smiley went right up behind him and stared straight into his facemask. Willy was so startled he flew up, hitting his head on the bottom of the boat knocking his mouthpiece out of his mouth, there were bubbles everywhere and he was in a real panic! The boys had never seen anyone move so fast. Willy's head came up out of the water, frantically calling for Jack to pull him back into the boat. "Quickly!" he shouted, "there's a shark down there! He nearly had me!"

The crew pulled Willy back on board, he was so relieved to be back on the deck. "Well, what happened?" asked Jack the ferret. "I don't know" said Willy, "I'm not sure, I was trying to get the rope from around the propeller when suddenly this huge eye was looking at me through my goggles. It made me jump and I hit my head on the bottom of the boat, making me lose my mouthpiece, whatever it was it nearly frightened me to death. There's no way I'm going back in with that thing down there!" At that moment Smiley popped his head up at the side of their boat, making a long chattering noise as if he was laughing at them. "Look!" shouted Jack, "it was that dolphin all the time!" he turned to Willy and said in a very angry tone "Can't you tell the difference between a Shark and a Dolphin?" Willy was

86

furious, and he shouted down at Smiley shaking his fist at him, calling him all sorts of names. The boys looked on, almost falling overboard as they rolled with laughter. By now it was too late for the Morning Star to do anything. The net was only a matter of a few yards away from the stern of their boat. Willy couldn't try to free the rope again in case he got caught up in the net himself.

He and Jack just stood there, wondering what to do next. Smiley decided it was time for him to get out of the way and avoid the net by diving down deeper. Once clear he swam back up towards the Acorn. The net was beginning to wrap itself around the back of the Morning Star. In a last minute attempt Keith, Willy and Jack were trying to pull the net in by hand, but they were only making things worse. They weren't able to pull it in fast enough and it was becoming more and more tangled around the rudder and propeller. They tried pushing it away with the only thing they had - the sweeping brushes used to wash off the decks! Surprise, surprise these also became entangled! The boys felt triumphant, but they couldn't help feeling sorry for Keith, they hoped they hadn't caused any damage to his boat. Just then Keith called them on the radio. Denzil up the microphone, "Yes, this is Denzil here, what can I do for you?"

They were expecting Keith to be angry with them, but to their surprise he congratulated them on a fine piece of manoeuvring. He said, he thought Smiley was the cleverest fish he'd ever seen! Denzil asked how Willy and Jack had taken it. "Not very well" was Keith's reply. "They're out on the deck now arguing with each other!" They all had a good laugh at this, and once again the boys apologised for tangling up the net around Keith's

87

boat. "Don't worry," said Keith, "I wouldn't have missed this for the world. I have a contract with Willy Johns saying they are responsible for any repair bills, even towing fees. So don't go away, we'll probably need a tow back into Newlyn. I'll give you a call in a moment when I've told Willy and Jack you will have to give us a tow back in – that will make them happy!" he laughed and signed off.

An hour passed before Willy and Jack had helped Keith pull most of the tangled net back onto the boat. There was still plenty tangled around the rudder and propeller but they would have to wait until they were in the harbour to free it. Keith came back on the radio, Denzil picked up the microphone, "Willy Johns wants to know how much it is going to cost him for you to tow us back into Newlyn." "Do they intend to carry on trying to catch the dolphin?" replied Denzil. There was a pause as Keith asked Willy and Jack, Denzil's question. "Yes" was the stern reply from Willy, "we are going to catch that dolphin, and he will be coming home with us." "Yes, it looks like it" said Keith. "How long do you think it will take before you have untangled everything from the boat," asked Denzil. "Oh, couple of days I would think." replied Keith. "We would need to do it at low water, when the boat is high and dry." "Will Willy be paying you for those days you have lost?" asked Denzil. "No, they only pay me when the boat is out working at sea." said Keith. "Well in that case," replied Denzil "you tell Willy Johns we want two hundred pounds to tow to you back in. Then tell him when he makes out the cheque to put your name on it and you keep it to make up for the two days we have lost you while the net is being freed from your boat." "I'll tell them," said Keith "but I don't think they're going to be very happy."

"Good!" said Denzil. Keith went out onto the deck where Willy and Jack were having a cup of tea. "Well," said Jack, "How much do they want?" "Two hundred pounds," said Keith. Willy was just about to swallow a mouthful of tea, he nearly choked on it when he heard the price! "You tell them we'd rather row back in before we pay them that much!" said Jack angrily. "I wouldn't be too hasty if I were you." advised Keith. "If we have to radio Newlyn to ask another boat to come out and tow us in, it will cost a lot more than that." Jack and Willy were bursting with frustration, knowing they would have to accept the boys' offer and their conditions. "Oh, alright!" said Jack reluctantly, tell them we agree. Just get us back into the harbour so we can get this mess sorted out." Keith radioed back to Denzil, "Yes, they are in agreement, they'll pay the two hundred pounds." "Right" said Denzil "we'll make our way over to you, we've got plenty of rope on board. When we're close enough I'll throw you a tow line." Keith acknowledged and signed off.

Jago went on deck and made ready with the rope. As they got nearer to Morning Star, he threw one end of the rope to Willy, who was on the foredeck waiting to catch it. Once he had hold of it he secured it to the forward Samson post. The Acorn slowly pulled away from them and Jago carefully fed the rope out over their stern, making sure there was never too much in the water in case it got caught on around Acorns' propeller. If that were to happen, well, then they'd all be in trouble! When you are towing a boat, one behind the other, the rope needs to be long. Jago tied the other end of the rope to the Acorns' stern post and it began to tighten with the strain. Denzil pushed the throttle forward and the Acorn surged forward and they were on their way back to Newlyn. All the way back Smiley kept them entertained, he gave them his full repertoire of tricks! He performed right alongside the Morning Star, as if he was trying to show them how clever he was, letting them know they had no chance of catching him today or any other day! Jack and Willy sat on deck watching him, mesmerised by his acrobatics. As they watched they were beginning to realise it was very unlikely if they would ever be able to catch him. But the thought of all the money he could make at their Zoo kept them thinking of new ways they could try and catch him.

As they grew nearer to Newlyn harbour entrance, Smiley came alongside the Acorn. "You really shouldn't show off like that you know, you're only going to encourage them to try to capture you." advised Jago. Smiley nodded his head back and forth saying "No." "Well, said Jago, "I hope you know what you're doing." Smiley nodded his reply, this time it was 'Yes', and he gave a small chirping chuckle. "You must keep a close watch on what Willy and Jack are going to do next." Smiley nodded his agreement and dived down into the water. He reappeared alongside Morning Star and with his usual huge belly flop sent a great slash of water showering over Willy and Jack, soaking them all over again! Smiley was really giving them a hard time and it was beginning to show in their faces. They looked depressed and sorry for themselves as the water ran down their faces!

The Acorn was approaching the quay, Denzil slowed down a little to allow the Morning Star to glide gently along onto the quay wall without bumping her sides against the wooden baulks. Her ropes were tied off onto the quay and she was now secure against the wall. Jago pulled the tow rope back in over the stern and Denzil turned the Acorn around and they headed back toward their moorings on the other side of the harbour. As they were tying off the Acorn to their mooring they could see their fathers rowing out towards them on a dingy. Treeve and Pirran had been listening to what had been going on their radio in the boatshed and had come down to see what it was all about. They tied their dingy to the Acorn and climbed abroad. For the next few hours they all sat together, listening as the boys told them all about the day's events.

Chapter 11

When the boys arrived at the harbour next morning they went over to the Morning Star to see what they were up to. As they approached her they could see all her crew were very busy pulling the tangled net up onto the quay. There were air bubbles coming up through the water, they assumed this was Willy John diving under the boat to free the propeller. Jack Evans was sat on the gunnels looking over the side, watching the bubbles rise. "Good morning" shouted Denzil! "Don't you give me any good morning!" was the very bad tempered reply. "All that rope around the propeller was your doing." "I don't know what you mean." said Denzil, tongue in cheek. "Do you know what he's talking about, Jago?" "Haven't got a clue" replied Jago, hiding the smile that was struggling to spread across his face! "Don't you give me that!" snapped Jack, "I don't know how you did it but I'm sure it was you two!" "Not very friendly today is he?" said Denzil to Jago. "You just be careful and stay out of our way. We'll be back out there soon and next time we'll have the dolphin. You just wait and see!" "We'll see." said Jago as they walked away unable to contain their laughter any longer. As they left Jack was still growling at them from the Morning Star.

The boys decided this would be a good time to top up the fuel tank on the Acorn. They rowed over to her and let go her mooring ropes, slowly they made their way across the harbour to the fuel line on the old quay. It didn't take long to fill the tank because the boys never allowed it to go down below half full. They returned to their mooring and spent the rest of the day washing down and cleaning the Acorn. By the time they had finished she looked as good as the day she was launched. All they had to do now was wait for the Morning Star to make a move, and try and find out what they planned to do next.

In the meantime they decided to go to the Fisherman's Mission and have a game of snooker. When they got there it was very full, most of the local fishermen spent their spare time in there. They sat drinking tea and telling each other yarns about their times at sea. The boys always felt a little uneasy walking in when it was so full, even though they knew almost everyone there, and those they didn't know knew their fathers. It was probably something to do with entering a mans world that made them feel awkward. After all they were still only fourteen and quite small amongst the old fishermen that were sat around. They were all tough men who had been hardened by the years they had spent at sea, they had a very distinctive, weathered complexion. Most wore faded denim fishing smocks, a few had large earrings dangling from one ear. To an outsider they would look like a proper motley bunch, but when you knew them they had hearts of gold and would be willing to offer help to anyone.

As the boys made their way through the crowd a voice called out their names, "Come over here boys, over here". It was Keith from the Morning Star. "Come and sit over here. I have just been telling everyone about your dolphin and what you both did yesterday". said Keith. "It seems most people are with you and don't want to see the dolphin caught, including me. So if you want me to stop taking Willy Johns and Jack Evans out, I will." Denzil and Jago thanked him but told him they would prefer it if he

93

continued to take them out, because if he didn't they would hire somebody else. At least with Keith they knew he was on the dolphin's side and that made it easier for the boys. Keith agreed and said he would continue taking the men out and help the boys however he could. "What are they planning next?" asked Denzil. "I think they're going to try the nets again, but this time they're going to cut them down in size, to about a hundred yards each. They think by scattering them around at random it will confuse the dolphin and sooner or later he is bound to swim into one of them. Yesterday Willy was so mad with the dolphin said he would use dynamite if he had to!" "Better not do that!" said Denzil determinedly. "Yes," agreed Jago. "What use is a dead dolphin?" "Don't worry," reassured Keith, "I don't think he meant it. It was seeing all their nets tangled up and you two charging him two hundred pounds to tow us in, it put him in an extremely bad temper!" "Even when he's in a good mood he's still miserable by other people's standards!" chirped in Denzil. Keith agreed he hadn't found him to be the most pleasant of people to work for and he felt sorry for the animals in their Zoo.

Denzil and Jago never did get the game of snooker they went in for, the older fishermen were busy telling them tales of their past adventures and now it was time to go home. Everyone wished them well and told them anytime they needed help to be sure and call them on the radio. It made the boys feel good to know everybody wanted to see Smiley free in the open sea. Next day, they arrived at the harbour at nine 'o'clock. There was a mist in the air and visibility wasn't very good, only about three hundred yards at best. The Sun was trying to break through the mist, as soon as it did the mist would clear. The Morning Star was still on her mooring along the quay wall, her engine was running and all the nets were neatly stacked in blue bins on the deck. "It looks like they're just about to leave." said Denzil. As he spoke they saw Jack and Willy come out of the cabin and start to untie the mooring ropes. "I think we had better get a move on, if they get too far ahead we might not be able to find them again in the mist," said Jago.

They hurried over to the Acorn. It didn't take them long to untie the mooring ropes and they chugged off after the Morning Star. Unknown to the boys Willy and Jack had decided to be smart. When the Morning Star left the harbour entrance they had turned left back along the outer harbour wall instead of right and out to sea as usual. They had realised the best way to find the dolphin was to follow the Acorn. The dolphin knew the sound of the Acorn's propeller and would make straight for it. So they lay in wait, out of sight until they could see the Acorn leaving the harbour. They didn't have to wait long, she came out of the harbour and as usual turned right and headed out to sea. Denzil and Jago scanned the water seaward but could see nothing. "That's strange", said Denzil "I didn't think the Morning Star was that fast. We should still be able to see them from here." "Perhaps not," said Jago, "They might just be on the edge of the fog." "Yes, you're probably right. We'll just keep heading out to sea. We're bound to see them soon." They were unaware the Morning Star was right behind them. She kept a safe distance between herself and the Acorn. The Acorn was just visible in the mist.

The boys continued out to sea for about another twenty minutes, still looking out for any signs of the Morning Star. "It looks like we've lost them." said Denzil, who was on the deck peering through the mist for signs of them. "Yes it looks like it," agreed Jago. "Is there any sign of Smiley?" asked Denzil. "No nothing yet. He's probably out there somewhere annoying Willy and Jack!" "Yes, more than likely," said Jago," I hope he'll be careful. With that amount of net on board the Morning Star, especially now they've cut it into pieces, it could be really dangerous for him." They didn't have to worry for much longer, within a few minutes Smiley was alongside the Acorn. His smiling face sticking out of the water looking at them. He gave them an excited chatter as if to say he was glad to see them. The boys leaned over the side and greeted him with their usual enthusiasm. Smiley came in closer and rolled over for them to scratch his belly, he seemed to enjoy that above all else! Suddenly Smiley rolled over and dived down into the sea. The boys knew something must be wrong. They looked around and could just make out a boat coming through the mist behind them. It was the Morning Star! "But how did she end up behind us?" asked Jago. "I don't know." replied Denzil," but they're up to no good, that's for sure." Willy and Jack were on deck with their binoculars, watching every move the boys made. "I think they're trying to sneak up on us." said Denzil," "Yes, but they've forgotten to take Smiley into account. He is able to detect our boat from miles away." added Jago.

Smiley was still diving in and out of the water alongside the Acorn not seeming very worried about the other boat, which had now moved in closer. "What have you got in mind?" asked Jago. "Before they can shoot their nets they have to slow down, if we drive around all day at eight knots they won't be able to slow down or they'll lose us in the fog. So they will

96

just keep following us round and round all day." replied Denzil. "Great idea!" said Jago. He called over to Smiley and told him to stay close to them as they were going to give the Morning Star the run around.

Denzil opened up the throttle and the Acorn lurched forward, they headed out to sea in a south westerly direction. Smiley led the way, gracefully diving through the waves. The Morning Star was only a few hundred yards away but she must have had to be near full speed to keep up. The speedometer on the Acorn was reading eight knots and land had long since gone out of sight. The boys reckoned they were about four miles out to sea now. They couldn't help chuckling to themselves as they watched Willy and Jack, still on the foredeck of the Morning Star with their binoculars fixed on the Acorn! "They must be getting soaked! "said Jago, as they watched the spray soaking the deck each time the Morning Star pitched into the waves.

This went on for about an hour and they were about eleven miles out and visibility was becoming poorer. Even though the Morning Star was only about a hundred yards away it was becoming difficult to see her through the fog. The boys knew if they went on much further they would be in the main shipping lanes, but Smiley was still in front of them and they felt sure he would keep them safe. All the same they thought it wise to slow down even if it meant the Morning Star would be able to catch them up. They reduced speed to half throttle and the Morning Star was soon alongside, Jack and Willy were on the deck, only about twenty yards from the boys. The fog was thickening, even though the boats were so close it was becoming harder to see each other. The Morning Star drew in even closer until they were almost touching. Willy shouted over, "You can tell that fish of yours he has had a reprieve for today.

The fog is too thick to mess about with the nets today." The two boys slowed down until they were almost at a stop, everything was still, just the sound of the two engines, slowly popping away. There's something about fog that seems to make everything go quiet. Just then Keith came out of his cabin and spoke to the boys, "I think we had better start making our way back in. If this fog gets any thicker we won't be able to see our hands in front of us."

As he finished speaking there was the loudest bang and crashing sound they had ever heard. It even made the boats shudder! "What on earth was that?" exclaimed Keith!" "I don't know," replied Denzil, "it sounded terrible, it couldn't have been that far away." Then both their radios came to life: "May-day, May-day, May-day. This is the Catherine Marie." The message was repeated three times, it continued, "We have been involved in a collision and we're taking in water fast. Our engine room is on fire!" They heard the coastguard ask for their position. The boys and Keith both rushed for their charts and as the Catherine Marie gave her position, they looked to see if they could see exactly how far away from them she was. Denzil decided to radio the coastguard and let them know they were very close to her. "Lands End radio this is the Acorn, do you read? Over." The coastguard replied; "Yes we receive you Acorn, but you will have to wait, we have an emergency on our hands." "Yes that's it," interrupted Denzil, "we are out here and we must be very close to the Catherine Marie, we heard the collision. The Morning Star is here too, we are going to start looking for them now." "Very good," replied the coastguard, "Stay on channel sixteen
98

and keep us informed on your progress. The lifeboat is on its' way from Newlyn. The Lizard lifeboat is also on its' way. We've lost radio contact with the Catherine Marie but when the lifeboats get closer they should be able to pick survivors up if she's still afloat."

Just then a bright orange flare could be seen faintly through the fog, it seemed to hang in the sky. "It must be a parachute flare" said Jago. Both boats immediately headed towards it but it died out quickly. Jago thought he heard something. He shouted to Denzil to stop the engine so that he could listen, he shouted to Keith to do the same. They all stood in silence, their eyes straining and their ears out on stalks. Then the word "HELP" drifted through the fog. Willy shouted out; "Where are you, we can hear you?" The voices seemed to come from everywhere, men and women, but the fog was so thick they couldn't be seen. The boats had to be very careful, they could easily run down the people in the water without even knowing. Then Denzil caught sight of something in the water. It was a young boy hanging on to a lifebelt. As he drifted alongside the Acorn, Denzil stretched out and grabbed him. Jago helped and together they pulled him aboard. He was shivering with cold but apart from that he was unhurt. They quickly wrapped him in a blanket and took him inside the wheelhouse where it was warmer. He was very frightened but he was going to be alright, he was safe now he was on board the Acorn.

The boy kept repeating the same thing over and over, "It sank straight away, it sank straight away!" The voices were still shouting for help through the fog, but they still couldn't be seen. Suddenly Keith shouted to Willy and Jack to help him, he had found somebody in the sea alongside the boat. It was a woman and under her was Smiley. He had brought her to the boat on his back. The men quickly pulled her in and Smiley swam off into the fog. It wasn't long before he was back, he'd found someone else! Denzil called the coastguard on the radio and informed him they'd found some of the people and so far they weren't hurt, just shaken up and frightened. He told them their yacht had sunk and everyone aboard was in the water. Just then the sound of foghorns and the powerful pounding of the lifeboat's engine could be heard. Denzil gave them a few blasts on his horn to let them know where they were, Keith did the same.

The number of people on board was growing. The Acorn had the young boy and a man of about thirty. The Morning Star had four people on board, all of them brought to the boat by Smiley. Jago asked the man they had on the Acorn how many people had been on board the yacht, "seven." he replied. Jago shouted over to the Morning Star, "There's one more out there." As he spoke the large blue bow of the lifeboat loomed out of the fog, "How many survivors have you got on your boat?" shouted the coxswain. "We have two and the Morning Star has four." replied Jago. Two of the lifeboat crew jumped down onto the Acorn. It was vital to get the survivors onto the lifeboat and into dry clothes before they died of hypothermia. The lifeboat crew didn't take long transferring them onto the lifeboat. The procedure went like clockwork.

Jago shouted over to the coxswain, "There is still one person missing." "No there's not" interrupted Willy "the dolphin has just brought him alongside the Morning Star." "Great! That's everyone and it looks like they'll all be alright," said Jago, with relief. The coxswain shouted back to the boys, "I don't know what you two boats are doing out here in fog like this, but one thing is sure, if you hadn't have been here these people would have died."

The Morning Star drew up alongside the lifeboat and Willy spoke to the coxswain, "It's not us you should be thanking for rescuing these people. The one we should all be thanking is the dolphin, he was the one that did all the hard work. He's the one who saved their lives by finding them and pushing them towards us." "What dolphin?" asked the coxswain, "where is the dolphin now?" Willy looked down into the water, expecting to see the dolphin there, but he had disappeared.

The three boats were side by side bobbing up and down in the fog. Willy called over to Jago and Denzil he told them after this experience, seeing all the dolphin had done to save people, both he and Jack realised how special this dolphin was and they were no longer going to continue trying to capture him. "I promise you both this will be an end to it. He's too special to be taken away from the sea, and from you. From now on we are on your side, the dolphin needs to stay free." He assured them. The coxswain of the lifeboat spoke, "I don't understand what was going on here with you two and the dolphin, perhaps you can explain to me when we get back on land."

Just then, as they were all looking down into the water, they could see something floating on the surface of the water, it looked like a brown linen robe and an old canvas bag! The coxswain told one of his crew to get the boat hook and lift them out and they would take them back in to Newlyn. These items meant nothing to Willie and Jack nor the lifeboat crew but they certainly meant something to Denzil and Jago! Their significance would mean even more to their fathers. This story is not the end but the beginning of plenty more adventures of Smiley and the Acorn.

MAPublisher Catalogue

ISBN/Titles /Image/Author	Description	ISBN/Titles /Image/Author	Description
978-1-910499-00-9 Father to child By Mayar Akash	This book about poetry of transition to adulthood. Ebook version 978-1-910499-02-3	978-1-910499-V4 Book of Lived By Penny Authors	This is the fourth Anthology - of poetry from different writers.
978-1-910499-14-6 The Halloweeen Poem by Zainab Khan	This is poetry book written by an 8 year old about their Halloween experience.	978-1-910499-36-8 Delirious By Liam Newton	This is the first of the Writer's Champion book getting Liam Newton's book of lyrics and poem.
978-1-910499-15-3 Anthology One By Penny Authors	This is the first Anthology - of poetry from different writers.	978-1-910499-39-9 Eyewithin By Mayar Akash	This is the 3rd book of Mayar Akash. The book catalogues the lost paintings by himself.
978-1-910499-17-7 Anthology Two By Penny Authors	This is the second Anthology - of poetry from different writers.	978-1-910499-37-5 My Dream World By Rashma Mehta	This book will keep readers spellbound as they read the stories, poems and lyrics wanting to know more looking into Rashma's dream world.
978-1-910499-29-0 Book of Lived v3 By Penny Authors	This is the third Anthology - of poetry from different writers.	978-1-910499-37-5 When You Look Back By Rashma Mehta	When you look back", who hasn't been there? No matter how strong you are, she manages to take you back to memory lane.

ISBN/Titles /Image/Author	Description	ISBN/Titles /Image/Author	Description
978-1-910499-50-4 **V5 Book of Lived** By Penny Authors	2019 release of the Penny Authors' anthology. This collection boasts a wider range of Poets with their "Lived".	978-1-910499-55-9 Riversolde By Meriyon	2020 release. Children's book based around fish life written and told through a poem.
978-1-910499-43-6 **My Life Book 1** By Mayar Akash	This is the first book of the author's entire collection of writing since the age of 12 to 43.	978-1-910499-54-2 **V6 Book of Lived** By Penny Authors	2020, the year of the Covid 19 issues, Penny Authors' anthology. This collection, Covid 19 experiences are encapsulated in their poems.
978-1-910499-44-3 **My Life Book 2** By Mayar Akash	The journeys are many and varied with so many challenges and obstacles as a Sylheti, Bangladeshi.	978-1-910499-49-8 Cry For Help By B. M. Gandhi	This is B. M. Gandhi's, (distant relation) collection of poetry depicting his life, Tanzanian life.
978-1-910499-52-8 **Lit from within** By Ruth Lewarne	This Ruth's collection of her poems keeping with the old school Shakespearian style.	978-1-910499-57-3 **The Vampire of the Resistance** By Ruth Lewarne	This is a rollicking tale of a reluctant heroine, forced into a world where she encounters high drama and low scheming, and not least of all, the Gestapo.
978-1-910499-69-6 **Consciousness** Mustak A Mustafa	Mustak's Collection of selective words from his conscious; inspired deep within.		

All books are available on-line, Google the titles and they will take you to the sites where you can acquire copies.